W

With the Flow

and

M. Bougran's Retirement

Joris-Karl Huysmans

Translated by Andrew Brown

ET REMOTISSIMA PROPE

100 PAGES

100 PAGES
Published by Hesperus Press Limited
4 Rickett Street, London SW6 1RU
www.hesperuspress.com

With the Flow first published in French as *A Vau-l'eau* in 1882; *M. Bougran's Retirement* first published in French as *La Retraite de Monsieur Bougran* in 1964.
This translation first published by Hesperus Press Limited, 2003

ISBN: 1-84391-050-0

CONTENTS

FOREWORD

For the English novel-reading public, Joris-Karl Huysmans is to all intents and purposes a one-novel author, and even that novel is more celebrated by notorious association than actually read. *A Rebours* (variously translated as *Against Nature* and *Against The Grain*) is the wicked book that corrupts Oscar Wilde's Dorian Gray, initiating him into the untrammelled pursuit of sensation in imitation of the book's hero, Duc Jean Floressas des Esseintes. During the first of the three trials which ended with him being committed to prison, Wilde was invited by the Marquess of Queensberry's defence counsel, Sir Edward Carson, to denounce Huysmans' novel. He fastidiously demurred – 'I decline to be cross-examined on the work of another artist. It is an impertinence and a vulgarity' – and the judge refused to allow Carson to pursue the matter. The non-French-speaking Victorian public must have speculated wildly about the book (not translated in full until the late 1950s) and its author. They would have been surprised and perhaps somewhat disappointed to discover that he was a clerk who worked for the Ministry of the Interior in Paris.

Huysmans' entire life and career is filled with paradox. His outer life was one of extreme circumscription, bounded by his labours for the ministry (for whom he continued to work until his fiftieth year) and cramped by the exiguousness of his salary; he was a martyr to his wretched digestion; he was timid in amorous matters, maintaining a long relationship with a woman who was the victim of a strange illness of mind and body who ended her days in a lunatic asylum; he was fussy, waspish and very proper in his behaviour. And yet from the time he was thirty, he moved in the most exclusive literary circles, befriended by Edmond de Goncourt (his idol) and Maupassant, advised and supported by Zola; he became a powerful and respected critic of painting; and he produced a series of novels which caused violent sensations of one sort or another as he worked out in print his slow journey from pessimistic realism to the most exalted and ecstatic form of Christian mysticism. Each of his novels is a Station of the Cross on the way to his final spiritual destination; each seems to contain a different world of expression and to point to new directions, from both the literary and the philosophical perspective.

The absurd and despairing *A Vau-l'eau* [*With the Flow*], published in 1882, occupies a very interesting place in the journey. It is preceded by three more or less realistic novels – *Marthe* (1876), a sober study of a prostitute, *Les Soeurs Vatard* [*The Vatard Sisters*] (1879), which portrays the lives of two working-class girls in documentary detail, and *En Ménage* (1881), the psychologically trenchant account of a bourgeois marriage, in which, as Huysmans' superb biographer Robert Baldick notes, characterisation begins to predominate over description. After it comes the spectacular departure of *A Rebours* (1884), with its exhaustive inventory of exquisite sensory indulgences, followed by *En Rade* (1887; *Becalmed* in the translation by Terry Hale), in which a couple retire to the country to find meaning and contentment. This novel is remarkable for its deployment of startlingly realised dream sequences, which led, some thirty years later, to its acclaim as a key work of the nineteenth century by the burgeoning Surrealist movement. In 1891, *Là-Bas* plunged its shocked readers into a vividly rendered medieval world of Satanism and sexual perversity. Then came the trilogy of novels in which the hero (fairly nakedly the author himself) embarks on the spiritual journey which takes him from monastery (*En Route*, 1895) to cathedral (*La Cathédrale*, 1898) and on to the further reaches of the numinous in *L'oblat* (1903), after which there were to be, and could be, no more novels; the journey had reached its destination. Huysmans' last work to be published in his lifetime was *Les Foules de Lourdes* (1906), not a novel at all but a study of the crowds of Lourdes; he had already written a hagiographical life of the Blessed Lydwine. As he lay racked with hideous pain from the terminal cancer from which, believing that it was possible to use one's suffering on behalf of mankind, he sought no relief, he was no longer inspired to write about spiritual matters. He had exhausted even God.

In the extraordinary trajectory of his work, *With the Flow*, the shortest, and in some ways the least ambitious, superficially at least, of his novels, has a curious place. It provides, among other things, a depressed self-portrait, or at least a portrait of the non-artistic aspect of his life, executed in the most severe of grisailles. Huysmans was proud to say that he came from a long line of painters; had he been a painter himself, each canvas would no doubt have been painted in a different style. Each novel he wrote has its own distinctive idiom; each employs a different technique. The symbolist-decadent luridness of *Là-Bas* is a million miles away from the ritual solemnity and carefully composed half-tones of *La Cathédrale*. (These two radically different books, incidentally, were Huysmans' two greatest bestsellers – *Là-Bas* playing on the fears and anxieties that filled the newspapers of the day with spine-chilling tales of occult excesses, as well as the prevailing paranoia about America's increasing domination of the world; *La Cathédrale* speaking urgently to French Catholics wavering in their faith. It was the massive sales from the latter book which finally enabled Huysmans to retire from the ministry.)

In *With the Flow*, Huysmans' habitual linguistic flamboyance (that style described by Léon Bloy, in Baldick's brilliant translation, as 'continually dragging Mother Image by the hair or the feet down the worm-eaten staircase of terrified syntax') is replaced by the monotonous voice of Jean Folantin, whose external life so closely resembles that of Huysmans himself: the poorly paid job at the ministry, the tedious colleagues, the poky quarters, the lack of a housekeeper, the occasional joyless encounter with prostitutes. Folantin applies himself methodically to the task of making his life more tolerable, doggedly trying to find a halfway decent restaurant, for example, or gingerly dabbling with religion; his efforts are inevitably doomed to failure. Boredom conquers all. Huysmans plays daringly with the reader's own boredom threshold, engendering a kind of exasperation which is held at bay by the suspense of knowing whether Folantin will, just this once, find some kind of satisfaction – one good meal, one enjoyable hour of rapture. He never does, though sometimes he seems tantalisingly on the brink of doing so. Finally, he resigns himself to being unable to affect his own life in any way: 'as he made his way back to his lodgings, he took in at a glance the desolate horizon of his life; he realised the futility of changing direction, the sterility of all enthusiasm and all effort; "You have to let yourself go with the flow; Schopenhauer is right," he told himself.' It is an unerringly precise account of the life of quiet desperation – defined by Thoreau as the experience of the vast majority of humankind – and the note it strikes is to be heard through a great deal of subsequent European literature: Laforgue, Hamsun, Ionesco, Eliot, Sartre.

The book was derided by its first critics, to Huysmans' intense delight. 'The newspapers are busy firing faecal bombshells at *A Vau-l'eau*,' he wrote. 'It gives them something to do, and it amuses me. How that book infuriates them!' Huysmans was no stranger to scandal and critical disapprobation. *With the Flow* had its starting point in a '*Poème en prose des viandes cuites au four*' ['prose poem about oven-baked meats'] which described the habits of life of a middle-aged bachelor, and appeared in the miscellany *Croquis Parisiens* [*Parisian Sketches*]. In addition to an evocation of the music hall, and studies of various typical Parisian figures, this collection contained *Le Gousset*, a sketch about a funambulist, in which Huysmans describes at some length the varied odours which arise from female armpits. The outcry was savage, again to Huysmans' unqualified delight.

But in France, at least, the book never lacked for admirers. André Breton, who idolised Huysmans, wrote eloquently of the unique quality of his writing, and one passage in particular appears especially relevant to *With the Flow*: 'Huysmans is a surrealist in pessimism... how grateful I am to him for informing me, without caring about what effect it would have, about everything that affects him, his preoccupations, his hours of gravest anxiety, everything external to his anxiety, for not pathetically "singing" his distress like too many poets, but for enumerating patiently, in the darkness, the trivial and totally involuntary reasons he still found for being, and for being, without ever really learning for whose benefit, a writer!... Fortunately the days of the psychological novel and all its fabrications are numbered. And there is no doubt that it was Huysmans who delivered the mortal blow!' (translation by Terry Hale).

For all its intrinsic merits, perhaps the most remarkable thing about *With the Flow* is that it formed the starting point for *Against Nature*. 'I pictured to myself a M. Folantin, more cultured, more refined, more wealthy, than the first, and who has discovered in artificiality a specific for the disgust inspired by the worries of life and the American manners of his time,' Huysmans wrote. 'I imagined him winging his way to the land of dreams... living alone and apart, far from the present-day world, in an atmosphere suggestive of more cordial epochs and less odious surroundings.' And it is true that M. Folantin is, in his own limited and plodding way, as much of a scientist in pleasure as Duc Jean Floressas des Esseintes. It is simply poverty which limits the terms of Folantin's experiment, as the last lines of *With the Flow*: '"So it's true: when you're penniless, there's no hope of ever getting the best; only the worst happens."' Des Esseintes ends up as unfulfilled as Folantin, and the reason is exactly the same: happiness is impossible to engineer.

There is another point of similarity between the two novels. Somewhat buried in both books, is the seed of what would only a few years later flower into Huysmans' discovery of faith. Significantly, the poet Arthur Symons called *Against Nature* 'the breviary of decadence', a point that echoes Huysmans' own description of *With the Flow* as 'a missal of minor misfortunes'. The religious terminology is hardly accidental. After reading *Against Nature*, Huysmans' friend Jules Barbey d'Aurevilly told him, as he had told Baudelaire after reading *Les Fleurs du Mal*, that he was faced with a choice between 'the muzzle of a pistol and the foot of the Cross'; Huysmans himself wrote to Zola that 'if you aren't a pessimist, you can only be a Christian or an anarchist; you must be one of the three.' Anarchism had no hold over

Huysmans, but his heroic traversal of the terrain between despair and redemption is an oddly inspiring one, and *With the Flow* is the most complete expression of that pessimism which, even at the start of the twenty-first century, remains central to our self-perception. Whether we will go the rest of the journey with him remains to be seen.

– *Simon Callow, 2003*

INTRODUCTION

On 18th October 1974, at half-past ten in the morning, the writer Georges Perec sat down in a café in the Place Saint-Sulpice, in the middle of Paris' Latin Quarter, and began to make a note of the things he could see through the window. The weather was cold and dry, the sky grey, with sunny intervals. He saw asphalt, trees, a flock of pigeons; buses (the 96 to Gare Montparnasse, the 86 to Saint-Germain-des-Prés); letters of the alphabet (a capital 'P' for car park); three tramps sitting on a bench in the square, swigging red wine; colours (a blue bag, a green raincoat); adverts (Danone Yoghurt, Société Roquefort); a coach full of Japanese tourists; etc. At twelve-forty he moved to the Café de la Mairie nearby and repeated the experiment, this time interspersing the mere notation of individual things with brief reflections on whole classes of objects (vehicles: cars – private, hired, driving-school) or activities (gestures when talking, waiting for a taxi, window-shopping). And so on throughout the day, in and out of a further two cafés, until seven o'clock. Perec's notes included the reasonably regular trajectories of the buses, the changing light, the sound of church-bells, the writer's own fatigue; etc. The next day, likewise, starting in the same café (insofar as one can step twice into the same café, or even once), gazing at the same square (ditto); it's true there are fewer pigeons around, and the buses no longer seem quite so fascinating, but there are two nuns who catch his attention, a girl carrying a tennis racket, and a wedding in the church of Saint-Sulpice, together with a man eating a cake ('no need to dwell on the fame of the local patisseries'), a man walking along with his nose in the air, a man walking along with his head bowed. And the next day, too: a rainy Sunday, so Perec muses on a tentative taxonomy of umbrellas (their shape, colour, material, the way they work), and watches people entering or leaving the church. 'Four children. A dog. A patch of sunlight. The 96 bus. It's two o'clock.'

This opuscule Perec published under the title '*Tentative d'épuisement d'un lieu parisien*' ['An Attempt at an Exhaustive Description of a Place in Paris']. In his Preface, he notes that many of the things in Saint-Sulpice Square have already been described, inventoried, photographed, recounted or listed in literature before. Perhaps the most significant literary precedent occurs in Huysmans' *With the Flow*. Jean Folantin, the ailing civil servant, finds in exactly the same spot as Perec a temporary refuge from the multiple dissatisfactions of his humdrum life. Like Perec, Folantin has lunch in a room with a view of the square, and sees many of the same things: 'people coming out of mass, the children walking down the steps holding their prayer-books... the whole crowd spreading out round a fountain decorated with bishops perched in their niches, and with lions squatting over the basin... people holding onto their hats and almost getting blown over by the fierce gusts of wind'. There are buses, fiacres (nineteenth-century taxis), 'huge yellow omnibuses from the Batignolles', a 'little green omnibus from the Pantheon' and a 'pale two-horse coach from Auteuil'. The weather, too, is grey, but there are gaudy splashes of sunny spells...

Folantin has known Saint-Sulpice from childhood: 'his office was in this district, he had been born there... his family had always lived in the area'. His familiarity results in a jaded sense of having exhausted its delights; though it is also one of the few places where he feels – for a time – at home, the other two being the public baths, and his own solitary bed. Then again, as Baudelaire had noted in his poem '*Le Cygne*' ['The

Swan'], 'the shape of a city changes more rapidly, alas! than the heart of a mortal'; and even the conservative district of Saint-Sulpice, Folantin realises, is suffering from the inroads of progress. The grouches of this most splenetic of men sometimes seem surprisingly prescient: he particularly dislikes the 'Americanisation' of Paris, which threatens to destroy its intimate little streets and old-fashioned shops and cafés in favour of brash, anonymous uniformity (though his indictment of America in this context is a little unfair: it was the mid-nineteenth-century French 'Préfet de la Seine', Baron Haussmann, who under Napoleon III drove the boulevards through the medieval huddle that Huysmans' hero seems to feel nostalgic for).

Perec's encyclopaedic enumeration of things seen and heard flattens out, in a pointillist manner, the distinction between people, things, street signs, birds, or evanescent gestures. So does Folantin's, though here there is a more deliberate dwelling on the piquant juxtaposition of different registers, the promiscuous intermingling of body and soul, as when he sees a dyer's advert of two scarlet hats, probably those worn by Catholic cardinals, and thus, even though the advert is plastered over a public urinal, hinting at 'the splendours of religion'. If Folantin's contemplation of the scene is less objective, free-floating, and fragmentary than Perec's, it is because Saint-Sulpice is, to him, a complex area which provokes contradictory responses. First and foremost, it is a Catholic quarter (the area is still today, as in the nineteenth century, *the* place to pick up a missal, a chasuble, or a monstrance). On one level, this is a source of resentment: Folantin, a bachelor of limited resources and a chronic sufferer of dyspepsia, can't afford to eat in a decent restaurant, and in Saint-Sulpice it helps if you are a member of the clergy and can eat in one of the seminaries (or are wealthy enough to dine with the rich); but this also, tenuously and vaguely, makes Saint-Sulpice a source of potential consolation: the bread of angels might provide spiritual sustenance in the absence of real bodily nourishment.

However, the religious hint is not taken in this novel of 1882: we are still some years before Huysmans' own conversion back to Catholicism. While in later works, notably *Là-Bas*, his study of devil-worship and black masses, Husymans returns to Saint-Sulpice as to a supernatural battlefield, in *With the Flow* we learn that Folantin has 'long since exhausted the charm of this quiet spot'. Religion tempts him again, towards the end of the novel, when the death of his cousin, a nun, inspires in him a wistful longing for spirituality, but he is too passive to respond to these intimations. Even if he states that religion alone can cure his discontents, nothing happens. He continues to go with the flow, to drift downstream, concluding, with Schopenhauer, that life is essentially boredom or suffering, and that any attempt to change the situation will only worsen it. Even the epiphanic moment when cheap music reminds him – in an anticipation of the Narrator's *petite madeleine* in Proust – of his grandmother giving him a sponge-finger remains a latent possibility, explored no further.

Folantin is thus a *flâneur*, of the kind that attracted Charles Baudelaire and Walter Benjamin: someone who strolls through the streets of Paris, observing the passing scene, without taking part; or someone who is so absorbed in himself that he barely even notices the outside world. When he does, it is in those short bursts of tetchy preciosity that distinguish Huysmans' style, balefully noting every stain on a restaurant tablecloth. His disgruntlement occasionally takes the form of an almost surrealist heightening of perception, reminding us that the

Surrealists of the 1920s, and their heirs, the Situationists of the 1960s, were more inventive and interventionist *flâneurs*, capable of hijacking the goods on offer in the tawdry antique-shops, bric-à-brac emporia, and flea markets of the metropolis, and giving them new and subversive meanings. But when Folantin window-shops, he is a more typical inhabitant of the modern city; one who knows – and this is the melancholy of city life – that the visual stimuli around him are out of his reach: antiques or books or prints he cannot afford, adverts for things he has no use for, solicitings to which his only response is a weary, if slightly camp, disdain. But as Baudelaire in particular showed, although the *flâneur* is modern man (and it is essentially a masculine figure we are talking about) as passive and consumerist – exposing himself to stimuli in the hope that one or other will coax his jaded palate – sooner or later, in any city, he will encounter the plight of those for whom the idea of a consumer society is itself merely a distant mirage. Folantin thus registers a wary respect for the real down-and-outs in the most humble of chop-houses, whose extremity puts his own *Weltschmerz* into perspective.

Still, self-pitying or not, Folantin's suffering is real enough. Is it due to lack of money? This is the conclusion the novel reaches, with its reference to the 'poor' who can expect only the worst from life. But in Huysmans' later novel, *A Rebours* (a title which suggests going *against* the flow, exploring the perverse and the unnatural), the hero, des Esseintes, is wealthy enough to afford all he desires. The novel becomes a list of potential remedies; but still des Esseintes is prone to an incurable accidie. Folantin anticipates des Esseintes in the range of solutions he tries, from theatre-going to interior decoration. (In the twenty-first century, these men would have even more to choose from: medicines and drugs – a daily dose of a hundred milligrams of sertraline hydrochloride to replace Folantin's sulphates of protoxide – a spell of therapy, the strides of physical culture and the practice of sports such as tennis, football, running, cycling, swimming, flying, floating, riding, gliding, etc. But it is debatable whether, for all that, they would cease to waste and pine.)

Folantin sometimes seems a solitary version of the six characters in search of a meal who wander through Luis Buñuel's film *The Discreet Charm of the Bourgeoisie* (1972): every time they sit down at table, either in a restaurant or at one of their homes, they are interrupted by death, or war, or the law. Only at the end of the film does the corrupt Ambassador of Miranda (played with svelte man-of-the-world charm by Fernando Rey) seize on a leg of chicken and munch it hungrily as he is hiding under the table from the soldiers who have come to arrest him; and then he wakes up – for behold, it was all a dream – and goes straight to the fridge for a snack, helping himself, for once, instead of being served. Folantin doesn't even manage that much: his hunger, both physical and spiritual, is unsated. 'Try cooking for yourself!' the reader cries, on reading yet another dismal restaurant review. He has asked his society for bread and it has given him a stone; or rather, as in the opening lines, in place of the fine cheese he desires, he is furnished with something that looks and tastes like soap. Reading about Folantin's discomfitures is entertaining, and the swerve into surrealism (cheese as soap, an exacerbated metaphor) is typical of Huysmans' aesthetically mannered prose, able to register the baleful attention to the real world that Folantin's frustrations impose on him. But reading about a neurasthenic's flayed sensibilities doesn't entitle us to share them: even when the food is awful, art can only give us the menu, not the meal. Behind Folantin's saturnine hypochondria lies something the text can only suggest we taste for ourselves, since art cannot serve it up wholesale on the page: the bitterness of bourgeois civil society, which seems able to cater for all tastes, but for all its undeniable attractions still manages (perhaps because of all those it excludes) to leave one, as the French say, '*sur sa faim*': wanting something more, wanting something *different* – and not for oneself alone.

M. Bougran, in the other story translated here, is forcibly retired after years of conscientious labour in the civil service. He is akin to all the lowly pen-pushers who populate nineteenth-century fiction (by Gogol, Balzac, Dostoevsky, Melville, Poe). He takes his retirement badly: his job gave him what little identity he has. So he lovingly recreates his office in his own apartment, sets himself impossibly complex legal cases to solve, and even hires a superannuated office assistant to make the illusion complete. His failure is partly dependent on the contingent whims of his maid Eulalie, jealous that she is doing a real job where the pretend assistant, Huriot, just sits around waiting to be summoned, and yet earns more money. She has a point. But then the text is raising just that question: whose job *is* more worthwhile? Isn't modern life full of 'superfluous' men and women who nonetheless force themselves to work harder and harder? The vast population of scribes populating the civil service and spinning out endless verbal quibbles, as baroque in their contorted artificiality as the trees he sees in the Luxembourg Gardens: is their job *really* necessary? Is ours? By what criteria? Oh reason not the need... But perhaps we are all caught up in our own versions of Jarndyce v. Jarndyce. Bougran is pathetic in that he cannot reinvent himself once he is retired: the machine no longer does any useful work, but on it whirrs, unstoppably, in his mind, for he has internalised all the machinery of the law: he will be judge, he will be jury, he will be prosecutor and defendant – Jarndyce v. Jarndyce, indeed. But as well as being pathetic, he is tragic, and his fate provokes a recognisable frisson. His scrupulous care for the letter of the law has made him a writer: one who can find no Civil Code to tell him what to write, and is yet obsessed by the need to *get it right*, even in the absence of any definitive criteria. His is the quest for *le mot juste*: a parody (or is it so parodic?) of the agonies of style endured by a Flaubert, a copyist taking dictation from an unknown source that can never quite be heard correctly. In his last written words, he rejects an appeal – his own, perhaps. In this short piece, Huysmans has created a haunting little parable, a negative version of Melville's 'Bartleby, the Scrivener' and comparable with some of the fables of Kafka – that other connoisseur of office life – aware that anyone who pushes a pen or taps away at a keyboard is inextricably entangled with the Law, desperately trying to placate – *whom*?

– *Andrew Brown, 2003*

Note on the Texts:
I have used Joris-Karl Huysmans, *A Vau-l'eau*, from *Croquis Parisiens* (Paris: Stock, 1905), and *La Retraite de M. Bougran* (Paris: Pauvert, 1964). I have greatly benefited from consulting Robert Baldick's translation of *A Vau-l'eau: Downstream* (London, The Fortune Press, 1952), and his biography, *The Life of J.-K. Huysmans* (Oxford: The Clarendon Press, 1955). Perec's *Tentative d'épuisement d'un lieu parisien* is published by Christian Bourgois (Paris, 1975).

With the Flow

1

The waiter placed his left hand on his hip, set his right hand on the back of a chair, and swayed on one foot, pursing his lips.

'Well now, it's all a matter of taste,' he said. 'If I were in Monsieur's place, I'd ask for Roquefort.'

'Very well, bring me some Roquefort.'

And M. Jean Folantin, sitting at a table strewn with plates on which leftovers were growing cold, and empty bottles whose round bases imprinted a blue mark like an official stamp on the tablecloth, pulled a face, in no doubt that he was about to eat a dismal piece of cheese; his expectations were fully satisfied; the waiter brought a kind of white lace with indigo marbling, obviously cut out of a cake of Marseilles soap.

M. Folantin picked at his cheese, folded his napkin, stood up, and left: the waiter bowed to his back and shut the door behind him.

Once he was outside, M. Folantin opened his umbrella and started walking. The biting cold, cutting into ears and nose like a razor-blade, had been succeeded by the fine strop of a pouring rain. The harsh, glacial winter which had held Paris in its grip for three days was relenting, and the slushy snow was melting and splashing beneath the swollen, rain-sodden clouds.

M. Folantin was cantering along by now, dreaming of the fire that he had lit at home before going off to eat his fill in his restaurant.

Truth to tell, he was not altogether free of anxiety; quite unusually, that evening, he had been too lazy to rebuild from the bottom up the fire prepared by his concierge. A coke fire is so difficult to get going, he reflected; and he dashed upstairs, four at a time, to find that in his fireplace there was not a single flicker of flame.

'To think there aren't any cleaners or caretakers who can lay a decent fire,' he grumbled, and placed his candle on the carpet; then, without taking off his outdoor clothes, his hat still on his head, he pushed aside the grating and refilled it methodically, leaving room between the lumps of coke for the air to get through. He lowered the shutter, worked his way through several matches and a quantity of paper, and then took off his clothes.

Suddenly he heaved a sigh, as his lamp had started emitting deep burping noises.

'Oh that's just great! No oil! That just about crowns it all!' He lifted the lantern lid and gazed with a woebegone expression at the wick that he had pulled up to the charred crown, jagged with black teeth. It had been exposed to the air and had gone all yellow.

'This life is intolerable,' he said to himself as he looked around for some scissors; he repaired his light as best he could, then flopped down in an armchair and lost himself in his reflections.

It had been a bad day; ever since the morning he had been in a foul mood; the chief clerk of the office where he had worked for twenty years had told him off, quite ungraciously, for arriving later than usual.

M. Folantin had bristled and, taking out his round pocket-watch, had replied sharply, 'Eleven o'clock precisely.'

His chief had in turn pulled out from his pocket a real Big Ben of a timepiece.

'Eleven-twenty,' he had retorted, 'I'm as regular as the Bourse.' And with a contemptuous glance he had deigned to excuse his employee, expressing pity for the antique piece of clockwork he carried round.

M. Folantin took this ironic way of exonerating him as an allusion to his poverty and he answered back in no uncertain terms to his superior who, no longer prepared to accept the senile inaccuracies of a watch, drew himself to his full length and, in threatening and majestic terms, again reproached M. Folantin for his lack of punctuality.

His working day, having got off to a bad start, had continued to be quite unbearable. In the wan, dingy light that made his paper seem a dirty grey, he had had to copy interminable letters, draw up voluminous tables of figures and at the same time listen to the chattering of a colleague, a little old man who, with his hands in his pockets, liked the sound of his own voice.

On he went, reciting the day's newspaper in its entirety, and even adding his own pennyworth of wisdom, or else criticising the way the writers had expressed themselves and suggesting other turns of phrase that he would like to have seen put in the place of those he loftily dismissed; and he interlarded these observations with details of his poor state of health, which, he said, was nonetheless just a fraction better than it had been, thanks to his constant use of populeum ointment, and repeated ablutions in cold water.

Listening to these fascinating remarks, M. Folantin ended up getting in a muddle; the lines he was drawing on his sheets started to sag and the columns of figures began to stampede; he had been obliged to scratch out whole pages and overload each line with corrections – but it had all been a complete waste of time, as the chief had returned his work to him, with orders to do it all over again.

Finally the day had come to an end and, under a lowering sky, M. Folantin had had to trudge his way through the gusts of wind, splashing along in fondants of mud and sorbets of snow, towards his lodgings and his restaurant; and lo and behold, to add insult to injury, the dinner was awful and the wine tasted like ink.

His feet frozen, squeezed into ankle boots that had started to warp in the deluge and the puddles, his cranium white-hot under the gas burner hissing over his head, M. Folantin had hardly touched his food, and even now his bad luck refused to let go of him; his fire faltered, his lamp grew sooty, his tobacco was damp and kept going out, staining the cigarette-paper with a stream of yellow juice.

He was overcome by an immense sense of discouragement; the emptiness of his prison-like existence became evident, and, as he poked at the fire, M. Folantin, leaning forward in his armchair, his forehead resting on the ledge of the fireplace, started to look back over the *via dolorosa* of his forty years, halting in despair as he came to each station of the cross.

He had not exactly been brought up in the lap of luxury; from father to son, the Folantins had been penniless; the family annals did, it was true, include a certain Gaspard Folantin who, back in the mists of time, had made nearly a million in the leather trade; but the chronicle added that after squandering his fortune he had been left insolvent; the memory of this man was still vivid among his descendants who cursed him, citing him to their sons as an example not to be followed, and continually warning them that they would die in poverty just like him if they hung out in cafés or ran after women.

Anyway, Jean Folantin had been born in disastrous conditions; the day his mother's labour finally came to an end, his father's sole possessions amounted to a string of ten little silver coins. An aunt who, albeit no midwife, was expert in this kind of task, decanted the child, wiped him clean with butter and, so as to avoid the expense of lycopodium, powdered his thighs with flour she had scraped off the crust of a loaf of bread. 'You see, my lad, you had a humble birth,' Aunt Eudore used to say, after putting him right about these small details; and Jean was already resigned to the absence of any well-being in his future life.

His father passed away very young and the stationery shop he had been running on the rue du Four was sold to pay off the debts incurred by his illness; mother and child found themselves out on the streets. Madame Folantin found lodgings elsewhere and became a shop assistant, then a cashier in a linen drapery, while her son became a boarder in a lycée; although Madame Folantin was in quite desperate straits, she obtained a stipend and went short of everything, saving what she could from her meagre monthly earnings, so that she would later be able to pay the fees for exams and diplomas.

Jean realised what sacrifices his mother was imposing on herself and he worked as hard as he could, winning all the prizes, and compensating in the eyes of his bursar for the disdain that his situation as a poverty-stricken young lad inspired, since he was successful in all the competitive exams. He was a highly intelligent boy and, for all his youth, already of a sedate disposition. Seeing the wretched existence his mother led, shut away from morning to night in a glass cage, holding her hand to her mouth as she coughed, bent over her books, forever timid and meek in the midst of the insolent hubbub of a shop full of customers, he realised that he would not be able to count on any mercy from Fate or any justice from Destiny.

So he had the common sense not to listen to the suggestions of his teachers who kept pushing him in the hope of getting a feather in their own caps and gaining promotion, and by slaving away uninterruptedly, he passed his baccalaureate early, at the end of the fifth form.

He needed to find without delay a job that would relieve the heavy burden his mother had to bear; it was a long time before he found one, for his frail appearance did not plead in his favour and he limped on his left leg as a result of an accident he had suffered as a boy at primary school; anyway, his run of bad luck seemed to have come to an end; Jean applied for a job in a ministry and he was accepted, with a salary of fifteen hundred francs.

When her son announced this good news to her, Mme Folantin smiled gently. 'Now you're your own boss,' she said, 'you don't need anyone else any more; my poor boy, it was high time'; and her health, already fragile, grew worse from day to day; one month later, she died of the results of a heavy cold caught in the draughty cage where she sat, winter and summer.

Jean was left alone; Aunt Eudore had been dead and buried for a long time; his other relations were either scattered far and wide, or else deceased; in any case, he had never known them; at the most he could remember the name of a girl cousin who was at present living in the provinces, in a convent.

He made a few acquaintances and even some friends; then the moment came when they either left Paris or got married; he couldn't be bothered to form new friendships and, little by little, he gave up the attempt and lived alone.

'One way or another, loneliness is a pain,' he reflected now, placing lumps of coke one by one in his grate, and thinking back to his former comrades. How marriage came between friends! They'd been really close, they'd lived the same kind of life, they'd been quite unable to get by without each other; and now they scarcely said hello when they happened to meet.

The married friend is always somewhat embarrassed, as he's the one who broke off relations; and then he tends to imagine that you look down on the life he's leading, and when it comes down to it, he is convinced in all good faith that he occupies a more honourable status in life than that of a bachelor – so M. Folantin told himself, as he recalled the embarrassment and the hint of stand-offishness he had encountered in old friends he had bumped into since their marriage. It was all so very silly! And he smiled, as the memory of the companions of his youth inevitably took him back to the time he had gone around with them.

He had been twenty-two at the time, and found enjoyment in everything. The theatre struck him as a place of delight, the cafés as a realm of enchantment, and Bullier's[1], with his girls stretching out their lithe bodies to the clash of the cymbals, and kicking their heels in the air, inflamed him, for in his overheated mind he imagined them naked and could see, beneath their trousers and skirts, their flesh all moist and taut. A dense odour of woman rose amid the swirling dust and he would be entranced as he stood watching the fellows in trilbies cavalcading along as they patted their thighs. But he had a limp, he was shy, and he didn't have any money. Never mind: his torment was sweet to him, and just like many other poor devils, he was happy with very little. A couple of words uttered in passing, a backward over-the-shoulder smile filled him with joy, and when he was back home he would dream of these women and imagine that the ones who had looked or smiled at him were better than the rest.

Oh, if only his salary had been higher! Short of cash as he was, without a hope of picking up girls at a dance, he had recourse to the women who lurked in alleys, the wretched ones whose fat bellies drooped along the edge of the pavement; he would plunge along the passages after them, trying to make out their faces lost in the shadows; and the garish lighting, the horrors of age, the ignominy of their clothes and make-up and the abject little bedrooms did not put him off. Just as in the greasy-spoon cafés where his healthy appetite made him devour the cheapest cuts of meat, the hungers of his flesh were such that he was all too happy to pick up the leftovers of love. Indeed, there were evenings when, penniless and so without any hope of finding satisfaction, he would hang around in the rue de Buci, the rue de l'Egout, the rue du Dragon, the rue Neuve-Guillemin, the rue Beurrière, just so that he might rub shoulders with this woman or that; he was happy to be invited over, and when he knew one of these women touting for trade, he would chat with her, passing the time of day, then withdraw with a 'goodnight', discreetly, so as not to frighten off the punters; and he longed for the end of the month, promising himself that as soon as he'd been paid, he'd have a rare old time.

Happy days! To think that now he was a bit better off, now he could graze in richer pastures and take his fill of exercise between cleaner sheets, he no longer felt tempted by anything! The money had come along too late, at a time when no pleasure could allure him.

But there had been an intermediary period, between being overwhelmed by the turbulence of his blood, and then, stricken with apathy, sitting impotently in an armchair by his fireside. Around the age of twenty-seven, he had found himself filled with disgust for the registered prostitutes to be found here and there in his part of town; he had felt like a bit of flirtatious banter, the occasional caress; he had dreamt of not having to get down to business on the sofa without a moment's hesitation, but of deferring his pleasure and sitting down at his ease. As his resources wouldn't stretch to keeping a girlfriend, since he was puny and lacked any of the social graces, any talent for light-hearted amorous chit-chat, or any gift of the gab, he had been able at leisure to reflect on the benevolence of a Providence which gives money, honour, wealth, women, indeed everything to some men and nothing to the others. He had been forced to content himself again with cheap and cheerful meals out, but as he was able to pay more, he was directed to the cleaner dining-rooms with whiter tablecloths.

On one occasion he had imagined he'd struck lucky; he'd made the acquaintance of a young working girl; she had condescended to give him more than just a hint of her affections, but, overnight, without so much as a by-your-leave, she had dropped him, leaving him with a painful souvenir which he found just wouldn't go away; he would shudder when he recalled that period of suffering when he still had to turn up at his office and had to keep on walking. It is true he was still young and innocent, and, instead of turning to the first doctor he could find, he'd resorted to quacks, paying no heed to the graffiti that were scrawled all over their adverts in the public toilets, comments that were perfectly truthful, like this 'will clean your blood' – 'Yes, and will clean out your wallet, too'; or perfectly menacing: 'Your hair will fall out'; or philosophical and resigned: 'You're better off sleeping with your wife'; and everywhere the adjective 'free', prefixed to the word 'treatment', had been crossed out, scratched out, dug out with a knife-blade by men who, it was easy to guess, had performed this task with conviction and rage.

But now the time for love was over, and his yearnings were suppressed; the pantings and the fevers had been succeeded by a settled and tranquil chastity; but also, it had to be said, what an appalling void had opened up in his existence now that his senses no longer raised their heads!

'This really is no joke,' reflected M. Folantin, shaking his head and poking the fire. 'It's freezing in here,' he murmured, 'it's a shame that wood costs so much; otherwise, what a fine blaze I could make!' And this idea led him to think of the wood they handed out left, right and centre in the ministry, and then of the civil service itself, and finally his office.

There, too, his illusions hadn't lasted long. At first he had imagined that good behaviour and hard work would lead to promotion, but he soon realised that patronage is everything; employees born in the provinces were supported by their members of parliament so that they still managed to get the best jobs. He had been born in Paris but there was no important personage to help him up, so he stayed at the level of a mere copying clerk: and he copied and recopied, year after year, piles of dispatches, drew up innumerable columns of figures, built up masses of records, repeated thousands of times over the invariable salutations dictated by protocol; his initial zeal started to cool and now, no longer expecting any rise or hoping for any promotion, he was slack and careless in his work.

With his 237 francs 40 centimes per month, he had never been able to move into comfortable accommodation, or take a maid, or treat himself and put his feet up, all snug and warm in their slippers. One day when he was fed up with it all, he had made an attempt to change things, flying in the face of all probability and all common sense. The failure of the experiment had proved decisive, and at the end of six months he had been forced to wend his way, yet again, from restaurant to restaurant, feeling he could at least be satisfied that he had got rid of his housekeeper, Mme Chabanel, an old hag, six feet tall, with moustachioed lips and obscene eyes set into her face over her sagging jowls. She was a sort of camp-follower who ate like a horse and drank like a fish; she was a lousy cook, and over-familiar to an impossible degree. She would plonk the plates onto the table any old how, then sit down opposite her master, hoist up her skirts and chatter away, laughing and joking, her bonnet askew and her hands on her hips.

It was pointless to expect her to serve him properly; but M. Folantin would perhaps have put up with even this humiliating lack of ceremony, if the amazing old girl hadn't stripped him of his possessions like a highway robber; flannel waistcoats and socks would vanish, old shoes would go missing, spirits would evaporate into thin air, and even the matches seemed to light themselves.

At the end of the day, this state of affairs could not be allowed to continue; and so M. Folantin screwed up his courage and, fearful that this woman would otherwise pillage him completely during his absence, he took drastic action and, one evening, gave her the sack there and then.

Mme Chabanel turned scarlet and her mouth fell open, revealing a toothless chasm; then she started to wave her arms about like a flustered hen. Whereupon M. Folantin amiably said, 'Since I won't be eating at home any more, I'd rather you used up the food that's left rather than letting it go to waste; so if you don't mind, we can look over it together and see what I've got.'

And he opened the cupboards.

'This is a bag of coffee and this bottle contains brandy – am I right?'

'Yes, Monsieur, it does indeed,' Mme Chabanel had groaned.

'Well, it's good enough to keep, and I'll hold onto it,' said M. Folantin. He said the same about everything else; Old

Mother Chabanel ended up taking away nothing more than twopence worth of vinegar, a handful of grey salt and a little glass of lamp oil.

'Phew!' M. Folantin had exclaimed as the woman trudged downstairs, stumbling on every step; but his joy had soon died away; ever since then, domestic affairs had gone all awry. Widow Chabanel had been replaced by the concierge, who pummelled the bedclothes into shape with his fists, and made pets of the spiders, whose webs he looked after.

Ever since then, M. Folantin's victuals had been both dubious and nondescript; he had been forced to do the rounds of the local eateries day after day, and his stomach had rusted up; now the time had come for Alka-Seltzer and indigestion tablets, and mustard to disguise the gamy taste of the meat and spice up the gravy that tasted like washing-up water.

As he ran through the whole sequence of these memories, M. Folantin fell into a terrible fit of depression. For years he had valiantly put up with solitude, but on this particular evening he admitted he was beaten; he regretted the fact that he had never got married, and he turned against himself the arguments he had trotted out when he went around preaching celibacy for poor people. 'So what if children came along? They'd bring them up, they'd tighten their belts a bit. Damn it, I'd do what everyone else does, I'd buckle down to it and take on extra copying in the evenings, so my wife could afford some decent clothes; we'd eat meat only at lunchtime, and like most modest households we'd be happy with a bowl of soup for our evening meal. What do all the privations matter in comparison with an organised existence? With the evenings spent in the company of your wife and child, with food, not copious but wholesome enough, with clothes mended, linen laundered and brought back at regular times! – Ah, a decent laundry service: music to a bachelor's ears! – Right now, they only come with my clothes when they have the time and they bring my shirts back all crumpled and off-white, my handkerchiefs in tatters, and my socks as full of holes as a sieve; and they laugh in my face when I complain! – And then, how will it all end? In the hospice or the asylum, if the illness lingers on; here at home, dependent on the pity of a sick-nurse, if death comes more quickly.

'Too late… my virility has gone, marriage is out of the question. There's no doubt about it: I'm a failure. Ah well, the best I can do,' sighed M. Folantin, 'is to turn in and go to sleep.' And as he pulled back his blankets and arranged his pillows, a prayer of thanksgiving rose from his soul, in celebration of the tranquillising benefits of his ever-welcoming bed.

2

Neither the next day, nor the day after that, did M. Folantin's gloom lift; he let himself go with the flow, incapable of reacting against this crushing fit of the spleen. Mechanically, beneath the rainy sky, he would trudge to his office, come home, eat, and go to bed at nine o'clock, to start up a similar routine all over again the following day; little by little, he slipped into an absolute numbness of spirit.

Then, one fine morning, he had an awakening. It seemed to him as if he were emerging from a period of lethargy; the weather was clear and the sun was shining on his windows with their damascene filigree of frost; winter was back, but it was bright and dry; M. Folantin got up, murmuring, 'Good heavens, there's a nip in the air!' He felt much more cheerful. 'Never mind all that,' he said to himself, 'I ought to find a cure for my attacks of hypochondria.'

After long deliberation, he decided he wouldn't go on living like this any more, all shut away; he would change restaurants. Still, even if these resolutions were easy to make, they were much more difficult to put into practice. He was living in the rue des Saints-Pères and there weren't many restaurants there. The Sixth arrondissement was a pitiless environment for a bachelor. If you wanted to live in the labyrinth of streets around the Church of Saint-Sulpice you had to have taken holy orders to find the right resources, the special dinners at *tables d'hôtes* reserved for men of the cloth. Outside religion there was no decent grub to be had, unless you were rich and could frequent the smart establishments; M. Folantin did not fulfil these conditions and so had to limit himself to taking his meals in the few chop-houses that were scattered around in his neighbourhood. It definitely seemed that this part of town was inhabited only by men with wives or mistresses. 'If only I could summon up the will to leave!' M. Folantin would occasionally sigh. But his office was in this district, he had been born here, what's more, and his family had always lived in the area; all his memories were attached to this old, quiet spot, already disfigured by the inroads being made by new streets, by the dismal boulevards – roasting in the summer and freezing in the winter – by gloomy avenues which had Americanised the whole appearance of the district and forever destroyed its intimate allure, without having endowed it in return with any advantages in the way of comfort, gaiety, or liveliness.

M. Folantin kept telling himself he'd have to cross the river to find a place for dinner, but a deep sense of revulsion seized him each time he strayed beyond the Left Bank; on top of that, he found it difficult to walk with his gammy leg, and he abhorred the omnibuses. In the end, the idea of having to undertake a long journey in the evenings in search of food made his flesh creep. He preferred to try out all the wine-shops and all the cheap restaurants he hadn't yet patronised in the vicinity of his lodgings.

Whereupon he deserted the greasy spoon in which he usually ate; at first he haunted the cheap restaurants, making do with waitresses whose uniforms, like those of nuns, make one think of a hospital refectory. He dined there for a few days, and his hunger, already given a frigid welcome by the rank smell of burnt fat that hung in the air, rebelled at the idea of tackling tasteless slabs of meat made even more bland by a poultice of endives and spinach. What a mournful impression was created by those cold marble counters, those doll-sized tables, that unvarying menu, those microscopic portions, those tiny mouthfuls of bread! Squeezed together in two rows facing each other, the customers seemed to be playing chess, moving their knives and forks, their bottles and their glasses, into the spaces of their opposite numbers, as there was so little room; and, his nose stuck in a newspaper, M. Folantin envied the solid jaws of his partners chomping on the gristle of the sirloin steak whose flesh resisted the probing of their forks. Feeling nauseous at the thought of the roasts, he fell back on eggs; he asked for them to be served fried and well done; generally they were brought to him almost raw and he forced himself to mop up the runny white with a few crumbs of bread, using a teaspoon to extract the yoke from the sea of mucus in which it was drowning. It was horrible, it was expensive and above all it was depressing. That's enough of that, M. Folantin said to himself; let's try something else.

But it was the same everywhere; every feeding-trough he tried had its own particular drawback; at the high-class wine-shops the food was better, the wine less rough, the portions more generous, but as a general rule, the meal lasted a good two hours, the waiter was kept busy serving the drunkards propping up the counter downstairs; and anyway, in this deplorable district, they served quite humble fare, cutlets and beefsteaks that cost you an arm and a leg because, so as to keep you away from the working-class men, the proprietor would shut you away in a separate room where he would light two brackets of gas.

Finally, as he worked his way down and started frequenting the really bad taverns and the lowest dives, he found the company repulsive and the dirt stupefying; the meat was tough and stinking, the glasses still bore the imprints of wet round lips, the knives were unpolished and greasy, and the threadbare tablecloths were stained with the remnants of egg-yolks.

M. Folantin asked himself whether the change was worthwhile, given that the wine was everywhere laced with litharge and diluted with pump-water, the eggs were never done the way you wanted, the meat was always tough and dry, the boiled vegetables were of a kind not even convicts in gaol would touch; but he persisted ('If I keep looking, maybe I'll find somewhere'), and he continued to prowl through the taverns and small restaurants; but instead of diminishing, his weariness grew heavier, especially when, making his way downstairs from his lodgings, he sniffed the smell of soup in the stairwell, saw the rays of light under the doors, met people coming up from the cellar carrying bottles, and heard footsteps busily trotting from room to room; everything, including the perfume that emanated from the lodge of his concierge, sitting there with his elbows on the table, the peak of his cap dimmed by the steam rising from his bowl of soup, rekindled his regrets. He almost started to feel sorry that he had thrown out Old Mother Chabanel, that battle-hardened trooper. 'If I'd been able to afford it, I'd have kept her on, despite her appalling behaviour,' he said to himself.

And he started to despair, for to his mental pain was now added physical decrepitude. As he no longer ate properly, his health, already frail, began to founder. He put himself on iron supplements, but all the warlike concoctions he swallowed merely turned his entrails black, without any appreciable results. Then he adopted arsenic, but Fowler's potion ruined his stomach and didn't fortify him at all; finally, as a last resort, he used quinquina preparations which set his guts on fire; then he mixed them all up together, blending the different substances, but it was a waste of time; his whole salary went into buying medicine; his lodgings were filled with masses of boxes, sample bottles, and phials; there was a whole pharmacy in his bedroom, containing all the citrates, the phosphates, the protocarbonates, the lactates, the sulphates of protoxide, the iodides and the iron proto-iodides, Pearson's liquors, Devergie's solutions, Dioscorides' salts, arsenate of soda pills and golden arsenate, tonic wines with gentian and quinine, coca and columbo.

'To think all this is just a joke, a complete waste of time,' sighed M. Folantin, gazing pitifully at all these useless purchases, and the concierge, while not having any say in the matter, shared his opinion – but he just went on dusting the room, in an even more desultory fashion than before, feeling an increasing sense of contempt, hale and hearty as he himself was, at the thought of this emaciated tenant who could only keep himself alive by swallowing drugs.

Meanwhile, M. Folantin's life continued its monotonous course. He hadn't managed to summon the strength to go back to his first restaurant; on one occasion he had got as far as the door, but as soon as he reached it, the smell of the grilled meat and the sight of a basinful of purple chocolate cream forced him to take to his heels. He alternated between wine-shops and cheap restaurants and, one day a week, he fetched up in a place that churned out bouillabaisse. The soup and the fish were passable, but there was no point asking for anything even slightly more substantial; the meat was as wrinkled as the sole of an old boot and all the dishes gave off a sour taste of oil lamps.

To whet his appetite again, dulled as it was by the vile aperitifs served in the cafés – the absinthe that stank of copper, the vermouths, the dregs of sour white wine, the Madeiras, the proof spirits mixed with caramel and molasses, the Malagas, the bottled prunes in wine, the bitters, and the cheap Botot water from the herbalists – M. Folantin tried a stimulant that had worked for him as a child; every two days, he went to the public baths. He enjoyed this exercise particularly because, with two hours to kill between leaving his office and having his evening meal, he thereby avoided having to go home to sit and wait, still shod, still clothed, watching the clock as he waited for dinner-time. And his first visits to the baths were delightful occasions. He would curl up in the warm water, and amuse himself brewing up storms and stirring up maelstroms with his fingers. Gently, he would doze off to the silvery sound of drops falling from the swans'-beak taps which created widening circles that broke against the walls of the bath-tub, jumping out of his skin each time the bells rang out furiously along the corridors, to be followed by the sound of footsteps and slamming doors. Then silence would reign again, broken only by the gentle dripping of the taps, and all the distress he felt would drift away; in his cubicle, wreathed in steam, he daydreamed and his thoughts took on the same opalescent hue as the water vapour, becoming affable and diffuse. In the end, everything was for the best; he fell into a stupor. Good Lord, didn't everyone have worries like him? At any rate, he'd steered clear of the most painful and most nagging of worries: those that came with marriage. 'I must have been feeling really low, the night I moaned about my bachelor life,' he said to himself. 'I really like being able to curl up between the sheets – just imagine being forced to keep still, to endure the contact of a woman year after year, and to have to satisfy her when I'd really just like to go to sleep!

'And then again, we wouldn't necessarily produce a child. If the woman were really sterile or took the proper precautions, there'd be no problem. But how can you ever be sure of anything? And if it happens, you have perpetual sleepless nights and endless worries. The kid starts howling one day because it's cutting its toothy-peg, and another day because it isn't; the whole bedroom stinks of sour milk and pee; and in addition you'd at least have to find a likeable woman, a decent sort of girl; oh yes, just try and find one, Jean! With my luck, I'd be sure to marry a real queen bee, or a little minx who'd never stop blaming me for her after-pains.

'No, let's be fair: every condition has its anxieties and its hassles; and anyway it's cowardly to bring kids into the world when you don't have much money! It means exposing them to the contempt of others when they grow up; it means throwing them into a disgusting struggle, defenceless and weaponless; it means persecuting and punishing poor innocents who are forced to start their fathers' wretched lives all over again. Ah, at least the generation of the unhappy Folantins will be extinguished with me!' And, consoled by these thoughts, M. Folantin could emerge from his bath, swallow down his soup tasting of washing-up water, and dissect his soggy, pulpy meat.

He struggled through to the end of the winter and life became more indulgent; his intimate existence indoors came to an end and M. Folantin no longer yearned so intensely for the cosy fireside where he could sit and doze; his walks along the quays resumed.

Already the trees were breaking into jagged little yellow leaves; the Seine, vividly reflecting the azure sky dappled with small clouds, flowed along in great blue and white patches which the *bateaux-mouches* churned into foamy swathes. The surrounding décor seemed to have been spruced up. The two huge pieces of stage scenery, the one representing the Pavillon du Flore and the whole façade of the Louvre, the other the line of tall houses extending as far as the Palais de l'Institut, had been given a good clean and a fresh lick of paint, so to speak, and the background, like a canvas stretched out all taut and fresh, set off nicely against its mellow ultramarine the pepper-pot turrets of the Palais de Justice, the needle-sharp spire of the Sainte Chapelle, and the gimlet spike and towers of Notre-Dame.

M. Folantin loved this part of the bank that extended from the rue du Bac to the rue Dauphine; he chose a cigar in the tobacco-shop near the rue de Beaune, and sauntered along, musing, one day turning left to rummage through the boxes on the parapets, another day turning right to inspect the shelves of the open-air bookstalls.

Most of the volumes piled up in the trunks were library discards, worthless junk, stillborn novels focusing on high-society women, and recounting, in the language of a gossipy old concierge, the accidents of tragic love, the duels, murders and suicides; others had a thesis to propound, ascribing every vice to the nobility and every virtue to the common people; yet others had a religious aim in view, they came gift-wrapped in the commendations of Monseigneur So-and-So, and sprinkled spoonfuls of holy water over the thick viscosity of their gluey prose.

All these novels had been written by people who were indubitable idiots and M. Folantin gave them a wide berth, pausing to draw breath again only when he reached the volumes of verse whose wings fluttered in every breeze. These at least were less dog-eared and less soiled, given that no one ever opened them. A charitable feeling of pity overcame M. Folantin at the sight of these abandoned collections. And how many of them there were! Veterans from the period when Malekadel made his grand entry into literature, and youngsters from the school of Victor Hugo singing of the mild month of Messidor[2], the shady woods, the divine charms of some young woman who in private life was probably on the game. And it had all been read in some select gathering, and the poor writers had been thrilled at being published. My God! They weren't expecting any resounding success, they didn't think they'd be bestsellers: they'd just wanted a discreet 'bravo!' from the sensitive and the well read; and nothing had happened, not even the merest ripple of esteem. Here and there a few insipid words of praise in some rag or other, a ridiculous letter from their master that they had piously preserved, and that had been it.

The saddest thing, thought M. Folantin, was that these unhappy souls were not wrong to execrate the public, for literary justice does not exist; their poetry is neither better nor worse than the poetry that sells, and earns its authors a seat in the French Academy.

As he mulled over these thoughts, M. Folantin, relighting his cigar, recognised the quayside booksellers who, talkative and weather-beaten, were standing, as they had the previous year, next to their boxes of books. He also recognised the book collectors who were trudging up and down the parapets of the riverbank just like last spring, and the sight of these characters whom he did not even know gave him great delight. He took a liking to all of them; he imagined them to be amiable cranks, nice, quiet people, passing noiselessly through life, and he envied them. If only I could be like them, he reflected; and he had in fact already tried to imitate them and become a bibliophile. He had consulted catalogues, leafed through dictionaries and thumbed through specialised publications, but he had never discovered any real curiosities, and in any case he could well imagine that possessing them would never fill that empty hole of boredom which was starting to yawn wider and wider in his whole being. Unfortunately, you couldn't develop a taste for books just like that, and anyway, apart from the out-of-print editions that his extremely limited resources prevented him from buying, there were hardly any volumes M. Folantin cared to procure. He didn't like cloak-and-dagger novels, nor adventure stories; he hated the pulp fiction churned out by Cherbuliez and Feuillet and their ilk;[3] he was interested only in the things of real life, so his library was restricted, fifty volumes all told, which he knew off by heart. And it wasn't one of his least causes of sorrow, the lack of books to read! In vain he had tried to get himself interested in history; all those complicated explanations of simple matters had neither captivated nor convinced him. He rummaged around at random, no longer hoping to turn up a book he could add to his collection. But his walk at least took his mind off things, and then, when he was tired of shaking the dust off books, he would lean over the parapet and gaze at the river; he enjoyed looking at the boats with their tarred hulls, their cabins painted leek-green, their mainmasts lowered onto the deck; he would linger there, entranced, contemplating the stewpan simmering on a cast-iron stove, out in the open air, the eternal black and white dog running up and down the barges with its tail coiled in the air, and the strikingly blond children sitting near the tiller, their hair falling across their eyes and their fingers in their mouths.

It would really be fun to live like that, he thought, smiling despite himself at these boyish longings, and he even had a twinge of fellow-feeling for the fishermen, sitting immobile like a string of onions, separated from each other by boxes of maggots.

On evenings like these, he felt better disposed towards life, with more sap in him. He would look at his watch and if it was still a while until dinner, he would cross the road, and walk down the opposite pavement, following the line of houses. He strolled along, continuing to dart a questing glance at the books whose spines were arrayed in the shop-fronts, going into ecstasies over the old bindings with their red morocco boards, stamped with golden coats of arms; but these were locked in glass cases, like precious objects that only the initiated can touch; and he would move on, examining the shops full of old oak furniture so well repaired that it had preserved not a single piece of its original wood, old Rouen plates manufactured in the Batignolles, great open Moustiers[4] dishes glazed at Versailles, paintings by Hobbema with their little brook, the watermill, the house with its bonnet of red tiles fanned by the breeze that wafted from a clump of trees wrapped in a haze of yellow light; paintings that were astonishing works of mimicry by a painter who had got into the skin of old Minderhout but was incapable of assimilating the manner of any other master or producing the least canvas of his own; and M. Folantin's gaze tried to pierce through the front doors to the depths of the shops; on no occasion did he ever see any customers; there was generally just a single old woman sitting in the jumble of objects among which she had found a little nook for herself; bored to tears, she would open her mouth in a long yawn that was copied by the cat curled up on a console table.

'It's funny, you know,' said M. Folantin to himself, 'how the women who sell bric-à-brac vary. The few times I've wandered through the Right-Bank districts, I've never seen any old dears like this one in the curio-shops, but when I've looked through the windows I've always caught sight of strapping young women, tall and attractive, thirty to forty years old, carefully pomaded and their faces plastered over with make-up.'

A vague whiff of prostitution emanated from these shops where the meaningful glances of the shopkeeper were designed to cut short the haggling of the purchasers. 'The old decencies are disappearing; in any case, the centre of the trade is moving out; now all the antique-shops and the better booksellers just stagnate in this district, and as soon as their leases expire they hoof it over to the other side of the river. In ten years from now, brasseries and cafés will have taken over all the shops along the quay! There's no doubt about it: Paris is turning into a sinister Chicago!' And, filled with melancholy, M. Folantin kept telling himself: let's make the most of the time left to us before the New World finally takes over with all its crass vulgarity! And he resumed his sauntering, stopping outside the windows showing off their displays of old prints, eighteenth-century pieces; but he was not particularly keen on the coloured engravings of that period or the engravings in the English 'black manner' which flanked them in most of the displays, and he longed for the prints of Flemish private life, now relegated to cardboard boxes, since collectors these days only had eyes for the French school.

When he was tired of loafing around outside these shops, he would, to vary his pleasures, go into the dispatch room of a newspaper office, a room furnished with drawings and paintings representing Italian women and oriental dancing-girls, babies being cuddled by their mothers, medieval page-boys strumming mandolins beneath balconies – a whole series obviously designed to ornament lampshades; and he would turn away, move on, preferring to look at the photographs of murderers, generals and actresses, all the people who were in the public eye for a week thanks to a crime, a massacre or a popular song.

But these exhibitions were, when all was said and done, not particularly entertaining, and M. Folantin, on reaching the rue de Beaune, felt more admiration for the ever-reliable appetites of the coachmen sitting at tables in the taverns, and his own hunger returned. Those platefuls of beef resting on thick beds of cabbage, those small, chunky platters piled high with Irish stew, those triangles of Brie, those brimming glasses, gave him pangs of hunger, and those people with their cheeks swollen by enormous mouthfuls of bread, their rough hands clutching their knives point upwards, their hats of *cuir-bouilli* that rose and fell in rhythm with their chomping jaws, all made his mouth water, and he would rush away, trying not to let this impression of voracity fade as he went; unfortunately, the minute he settled down in the restaurant, his throat would seem to shrivel, and he would gaze piteously at his meat, wondering what was the point of the quassia marinading in a jug of water in his office.

In spite of everything, this walk kept the blues at bay, and he drifted on through the summer, strolling along the Seine before dinner and, once he had finished his meal, settling down on the terrace of some café. He smoked, sniffed the fresh air and, despite his disliking for Vienna beers brewed with sap of aloes and box-tree water, more like Belgian beer than anything else, he would slowly get through two small mugs of the stuff, disinclined to go to bed.

Even the daytime, during this season, was less of a strain. Sitting in his shirtsleeves, he would doze in his office, listening distractedly to the stories told by his colleague, waking up to fan himself with a directory, working as little as possible, dreaming up new routes for his walk. No longer did he have to put up with the bore of having to leave his nice warm office, as he did in winter, or hurry through the streets to eat his dinner, his feet soaking, and then go back home to his freezing lodgings. Quite the opposite: he felt a sense of relief when he could escape from his office that stank with the familiar stuffy, dusty smell of boxes, bundles of papers, and inkpots.

And then, his lodgings were better maintained; the caretaker no longer had to lay in a fire, and if the bed continued to be roughly made and the sheets not tucked in, it hardly mattered, since M. Folantin could sleep naked on top of the sheets and blankets.

The thought of being able to stretch out alone, on those stormy nights when you sweat as much as if you were in a bath-house, tossing and turning in clinging sheets, also filled him with pleasure. 'I pity those who live with someone else,' he said to himself, as he rolled around on his bed, seeking a fresh place to lie. And destiny seemed to him, at times like this, more hospitable and less refractory.

3

Soon the period of stifling heat started to abate; the long journeys drew in, there was a new chill in the air, the mackerel skies lost their blueness, and became fluffy as if with mildew. Autumn would soon be back, bringing its fogs and rains; M. Folantin foresaw inexorable evenings and, filled with dread, he laid fresh plans.

First he resolved to break with his antisocial existence, to try out the *tables d'hôtes*, strike up an acquaintance with the people sitting next to him, and even to frequent the theatres.

His wish was granted; one evening, at the door of his office, he met a gentleman he knew. They had eaten next to each other for a whole year, warning each other off the unsatisfactory or poorly cooked dishes, lending each other their newspapers, discussing the virtues of the different iron supplements they ingested, drinking tar-water together for a month, uttering prognostications about the changes in the weather, and between the two of them devising different diplomatic alliances for France.

Their relationship had not gone any further. They would shake each other by the hand and turn their backs on each other once they were outside on the pavement, and yet the departure of this spiritual kinsman had filled M. Folantin with sadness.

He was delighted to see him.

'Ah, Monsieur Martinet!' he said, 'How are things?'

'Monsieur Folantin! Well… well… and how've you been all this time? It's been ages!'

'Ah, you're the one who abandoned me,' retorted M. Folantin. 'What on earth has become of you?'

And they caught up with each other's news. M. Martinet was now the assiduous patron of a *table d'hôtes* and immediately he started exaggeratedly singing its praises. 'Ninety to a hundred francs per month; it's clean and well run; you get to eat your fill, in good company. Why don't you come and dine there too?'

'I don't really like *tables d'hôtes*,' said M. Folantin; 'I'm not very sociable, you know; I can't bring myself to make conversation with strangers.'

'But nobody forces you to talk. It's like being at home. They don't all sit round one table, it's just the same as in a big restaurant. Look here, why don't you try – come along this evening.'

M. Folantin hesitated; he was torn between the attractive prospect of not having to take his meal alone and his fear of eating en masse.

'Come on! You're surely not going to refuse,' insisted M. Martinet. 'It'll be my turn to accuse *you* of abandoning *me* if, the one time I bump into you, you leave me in the lurch.'

M. Folantin was afraid of being impolite and he docilely followed his companion through the streets. 'Here it is. Up we go!' And M. Martinet stopped on the landing, outside a green swing-door.

A loud clatter of plates could be heard over an uninterrupted hum of voices; then the door opened and, to the sounds of a violent uproar, men with their hats already on came tumbling down the stairwell, rattling their canes along the banisters.

M. Folantin and his friend stood aside, then they in their turn pushed open the door into a billiard-room. M. Folantin fell back, choking. The room was filled with a dense cloud of tobacco, occasionally sliced by the cut and thrust of a billiard-cue. M. Martinet drew his guest into another room, where the fug was, if anything, even thicker; and here and there, amid the wheezing of choked-up pipes, the rattle of dominoes falling over, the bursts of laughter, individual bodies passed by almost invisibly, their presence deducible only from the displacements of vapour they caused. M. Folantin stood there, dumbstruck, groping around for a chair.

M. Martinet had left him. Dimly, through the clouds of smoke, M. Folantin saw him emerging from a door. 'We'll have to wait a bit,' said M. Martinet, 'all the tables are full; oh, it won't be long!'

Half an hour went by. M. Folantin would have given almost anything never to have set foot in this dive, where you could smoke but not eat. From time to time, M. Martinet slipped away to check whether all the seats were still taken. 'There are two gentlemen who are on their cheese course,' he said with satisfaction, 'I've reserved their places.'

Another half-hour went by. M. Folantin asked himself whether he wouldn't do better to slip off down the stairs while his companion was looking out for a table. Finally, M. Martinet returned with the news that the two cheese-eaters had departed, and they made their way into a third room where they sat down, packed like sardines in a tin.

On the steaming tablecloth, amid the splatterings of gravy and the breadcrumbs, plates were plonked down in front of them and they were served a tough and chewy piece of meat, some tasteless vegetables, a roast beef whose rubbery flesh bent under the knife, a salad and a dessert. This room reminded M. Folantin of the dining-hall of a boarding-school, but one where discipline was poor and the pupils were allowed to shout and bawl at table. All that was missing were the mugs with their bottoms reddened by abundant wine stains, and the plates turned upside down so as to form a slightly cleaner surface on which to spread prunes or jam.

The fodder and the wine were certainly wretched, but what was more wretched than the fodder, and even more wretched than the wine, was the company amidst which they found themselves chewing on their food; the skinny servant girls who brought the dishes, the gaunt women, sharp and severe of feature, with hostile eyes. You were overcome by feelings of complete impotence when you looked at them; you felt they were keeping you under surveillance and, your courage failing, you ate carefully, not daring to trim your meat or peel your fruit, for fear of a scolding, too nervous to help yourself to seconds beneath that gaze that sized up your hunger and forced you to hide it deep in your belly.

'Well – what did I tell you?' asked M. Martinet. 'A charming place, isn't it? And here you get real meat.'

M. Folantin didn't utter a word; all around him, a hideous hubbub was rising from every table.

All the races of southern France filled the seats, spitting and taking their ease, bellowing away. All the people from Provence, Lozière, Gascony, Languedoc, all of them with cheeks blackened by curly whiskers like shavings of ebony, hairy nostrils and fingers, and raucous voices, were roaring with laughter like madmen, and their regional accents, together with the epileptic jerking of their bodies, meant that their sentences were chopped and mangled into small pieces that were stuffed into your ears and split your eardrums.

They were almost all students, that glorious younger generation whose second-rate ideas reassure the ruling classes that they will always be able to recruit new candidates to replenish their own inane ranks. M. Folantin watched as every commonplace remark, every idiotic joke, every outdated literary opinion, every paradox made hackneyed by a hundred years of over-use, was paraded before his eyes.

In his view, an ordinary worker had more refined wit and a draper's assistant more polish. Either way, the heat was stifling. The plates and glasses were misted over with condensation; the doors as they were flung open emitted great warm gusts of tobacco smoke; herds of students continued to arrive and as they impatiently waited their turn, crowded in on the people still at table. Just as in the buffet of a railway station, you had to eat double-quick, and swill your wine down as fast as you could.

'So, this is the good old *table d'hôtes* that used to serve those starting out on a political career with their daily crust!', reflected M. Folantin, and the thought that these people filling the rooms with their bacchanalian revels would in their turn become solemn personages, laden with honours and plum jobs, made him feel sick.

'Stuff your face with cold meat in your own home, and drink plain water: anything rather than eat here,' he thought.

'Are you going to have a coffee?' asked M. Martinet, in a friendly tone.

'No thanks, I'm suffocating in here, I'm going out for a breather.'

But M. Martinet was disinclined to leave him. He caught up with him on the landing and seized him by the arm.

'Where are you taking me?' said M. Folantin, his heart sinking.

'Come on, my friend,' said M. Martinet, 'I can see that my *table d'hôtes* wasn't really to your taste.'

'Oh it was fine, just fine... at that price it was surprisingly good value... it was just very hot in there,' said M. Folantin timidly, afraid he might have hurt his host's feelings by his glum expression and his sudden flight.

'Well, we don't see each other often enough for me to want you to go away with a bad impression,' said M. Martinet cordially. 'Anyway, how are we going to kill time this evening? If you like the theatre, I'd suggest going to the Opéra-Comique. We've got time,' he said, casting a glance at his watch. 'They're playing *Richard the Lionheart* and *Le Pré-aux-Clercs* this evening.[5] What do you say?'

'Whatever you like.' After all – thought M. Folantin – I might even enjoy the change of scene, and how can I turn down a proposal from this kind chap, when I've already poured cold water over all his enthusiasms? 'Allow me to offer you a cigar,' he said, going into a tobacconist's.

They spent ages trying to get their Havana cigars to light, but had to give up in exhaustion. They tasted like cabbages and wouldn't draw. Another pleasure up the spout, said M. Folantin to himself; even if you're prepared to pay good money, you can't find a decent cigar any more! 'We'd do better to give up,' he continued as he turned to M. Martinet, who was pulling with all his strength on his Havana, which was starting to disintegrate, emitting the merest wisp of smoke. 'Anyway, we're here' – and he ran over to the kiosk and brought back two tickets for the orchestra stalls.

Richard was just starting. The auditorium was empty.

M. Folantin experienced, during the first act, a strange impression; this series of songs for the spinet reminded him of the music box in the shop of a wine merchant he had sometimes frequented. When the assistants set the handle turning, a ripple of old-time airs chimed out a very slow and very gentle melody, with the occasional high-pitched crystalline note dancing over the mechanical clatter of the ritornellos.

In the second act, he was struck by another impression. The aria 'A Burning Fever' brought to mind the image of his grandmother, singing the song in her quavering voice while sitting on the Utrecht velvet of her elegant sofa; and for a second he tasted in his mouth the sponge-fingers she used to give him when he had been a good little boy.

He ended up losing track of the play completely; in any case, the singers had no voice at all and they contented themselves with sticking their big round mouths over the edge of the stage, while the orchestra dozed off, tired of having to dust down and perform this lifeless music.

Then, in the third act, M. Folantin thought neither of the wine merchant's music box, nor of his grandmother: his nose was suddenly filled with the smell of an old box he had at home, a musty, vague smell, retaining a whiff of something like cinnamon. My God! How long ago all that was!

'Fine comic opera, isn't it?' said M. Martinet, nudging him in the ribs.

M. Folantin came down to earth with a bump. The spell was broken; they got up as the curtain was coming down, amid the acclamations of the hired clappers.

Le Pré-aux-Clercs, which followed *Richard*, left M. Folantin feeling unutterably depressed. In bygone days, he had been enraptured by the well-known arias; now all these romantic songs seemed to him hackneyed, and the performers irritated him. The tenor stood there on the stage like a floor-polisher and sang with a nasal twang – when by chance, any thin quaver of voice managed to emerge and dribble out of his mouth. Costumes, scenery, the whole performance was on the same dismal level; the piece would have been booed off stage in any foreign or provincial town, since nowhere else would such a ridiculous male soloist and such eccentric women singers have been tolerated. And yet the auditorium had filled up, and the public applauded at the passages to which the implacable band of hired clappers drew their attention.

M. Folantin was in real pain. He had fond memories of the *Le Pré-aux-Clercs*, and now they too were being destroyed.

'Everything's going to the dogs,' he said to himself, heaving a sigh.

And so, when M. Martinet, who was thoroughly enjoying his evening out, suggested they repeat the experience and indulge in similar treats from time to time – they could go to the Théâtre des Français together, if he felt like it – M. Folantin waxed indignant and, forgetting that he had vowed to keep his opinions to himself, declared in the most forthright terms that he would never set foot in this theatre again.

'Why ever not?' asked M. Martinet.

'Why not? Well, to begin with, if there was such a thing as an entertaining, well-written play – and *I* have certainly not come across one – I'd rather read it at home, sitting in my armchair; and secondly, I certainly don't need ham actors, most of them with no training, attempting to interpret the thoughts of the fellow who has entrusted them with the task of flogging his wares.'

'But all the same,' said M. Martinet, 'you have to admit that the actors of the Théâtre-Français –'

'Them!' exclaimed M. Folantin. 'Come off it! They're like the cooks of the Palais-Royal, good for mixing the sauces and nothing more! All they can do is drown the portions they are given in the same everlasting white sauce if it's a comedy, and the same brown sauce if it's a drama. They're incapable of inventing a third kind of sauce; anyway, tradition wouldn't allow it.

'Oh yes, they're so vulgar and uninventive, that lot! Still, you have to do them justice, they know all about the art of advertising – they've taken over from the smart clothes-shops the idea of a having a man standing prominently amid the wares, showing off his braids and ribbons and giving added lustre by his presence to the prestige of the emporium so as to bring in the customers!'

'But, Monsieur Folantin, but –'

'No buts! That's the way it is, and basically it's no bad thing I've been given a chance to express my opinion on M. Coquelin's[6] acting-bazaar. And now, my friend, I see I have reached my destination. I am delighted to have met you again. I hope to see you soon; I will look forward to it.'

The consequences of this evening were salutary. The memory of the exhaustion and discomfort he had endured meant that M. Folantin came to the conclusion that he would be happy to dine wherever he wanted and to spend the whole evening at home; he decided that there were advantages to solitude, and that sitting mulling over his memories and entertaining himself with his own idle musings was still preferable to the company of people whose convictions and likes one did not share; his desire to rub shoulders with people or nudge his neighbour's elbow vanished, and yet again he drew the same melancholy moral: when old friends have disappeared, you may as well give up looking for any others, resign yourself to living apart, and get used to solitude.

Then he tried to concentrate his mind, to take an interest in the least little things, to draw consoling lessons from the lives he saw around his table; for some time he went to take his evening meal in a cheap restaurant near the Red Cross. This establishment was generally frequented by the aged, by old ladies who would turn up each day at a quarter to six, and the tranquillity of the little dining-room made up, to his mind, for the monotony of the food. They looked like people without families or friends, seeking out dark corners to carry out some chore in silence; and M. Folantin found himself feeling more at home in this world of the disinherited – people who were discreet and polite, having doubtless known better days and more interesting evenings. He knew almost all of them by sight and he felt an affinity with these transients who hesitated before choosing a dish from the menu, who broke their bread carefully and hardly drank at all, dragging along their ruined stomachs and the wounded weariness of lives led without hope or purpose.

Here there were no noisy cries, no shouting; the serving-girls consulted the customers in low voices. But if none of these ladies, and none of these gentlemen, exchanged a word, all of them at least greeted one another gracefully, as they came in or went out, and in this cheap diner they gave one the impression that they were habitués of the salons.

'I'm at least luckier than all these people,' M. Folantin said to himself. 'They have perhaps lost children, wives, a fortune – once upon a time they could live with their heads held high, but now they've been brought low.'

As he came to pity other people, he ended up by feeling less pity for himself; he would return home and think that, all the same, his sorrows were not so very significant and his miseries merely superficial. 'How many individuals, at this very moment, are tramping the streets, homeless; how many would envy my big armchair, my fire, my packet of tobacco which I can dip into as and when I like!' And he would rekindle the flames of his chimney fire, toast his slippers, and mix glowing hot toddies. 'If only some really artistic books would appear in the bookshops, life would be, all in all, really quite tolerable,' he concluded.

Several weeks went by in this way, and his colleague in the office declared that M. Folantin was looking younger every day. M. Folantin had started to make conversation now, listening with angelic patience to all the gossip, and even taking an interest in his friend's infirmities; in addition, as the cold weather started to return, his appetite was behaving more regularly, and he attributed this improvement to the wines with creosote supplements and the manganese preparations that he absorbed. 'I've finally found a type of medication that's less unreliable and more effective than the others,' he thought. And he recommended it to everyone he met.

In this way he made it through to winter; but when the first snow fell, his melancholy resurfaced. He wearied of the cheap restaurant where he had been a regular since autumn, and he again started to browse round for another, sometimes in one part of town, sometimes in another. Several times he crossed the bridges and tried new restaurants; but in the crush, the waiters dashed all over the place, never responding to your appeals or else banging your plate down on the table and running off as soon as you asked for some bread.

The food was no better than on the Left Bank, and the service was arrogant and derisory. M. Folantin took the message to heart and from now on stayed in his own district, resolving never to stir from it again.

His lack of appetite returned. Once more he was forced to conclude how useless were the potions and stimulants he took, and the remedies whose praise he had so loudly sung went to join the others, on the shelves.

What was he to do? He could get through the week, just: it was Sundays that hung so heavily on him.

In bygone days he had idly strolled round the deserted parts of town; he enjoyed walking down forgotten little alleyways, poor, provincial streets, and looking in through ground-floor windows at the mysteries of ordinary households. But nowadays, the calm and silent streets had been demolished, the curious passages all torn down. It was impossible to look through the half-open doors of old buildings, to spot the edge of a scrap of garden, the rim of a well, or the corner of a bench; it was impossible to tell yourself that life would be less stressful and tumultuous in this courtyard, to dream of the time in life when you would be able to retire into this silence and warm your old age in an atmosphere less cold.

Everything had vanished; no more leafy bushes, no more trees, just endless rows of barracks stretching as far as the eye could see. And, in this new Paris, M. Folantin suffered an impression of anguish and malaise.

He was the kind of man who loathed smart shops; nothing in the world would have induced him to set foot in an elegant barber's-shop or one of those modern grocery stores whose displays are illuminated by hissing jets of gaslight; he only liked old, simple shops where you were received without ceremony, where the shopkeeper didn't try to throw dust in your eyes, or attempt to make you feel small with his wealth.

So he had stopped taking his Sunday walks through the garish display of bad taste that was invading even the suburbs. In any case, his strolls through Paris no longer had the tonic effect they had once had; he felt himself even tinier and more puny, more lost and more alone, when he was surrounded by these tall houses with their entrance halls lined with marble and their concierges' lodges arrogantly displaying all the posh comforts of a bourgeois living-room.

However, one part of his district was still intact, near the mutilated Luxembourg Gardens, and had preserved its welcoming and cosy atmosphere for him: the Place Saint-Sulpice.

Sometimes he would have lunch in a wine-shop whose dining-room was on the corner of the rue du Vieux-Colombier and the rue Bonaparte, and there, sitting in the mezzanine, he would look down over the square through the window, contemplating the people coming out of mass, the children walking down the steps holding their prayer-books, just in front of their mothers and fathers, the whole crowd spreading out around a fountain decorated with bishops perched in their niches, and with lions squatting over the basin.

As he leant out a little over the balustrade, he could see the corner of the rue Saint-Sulpice, a terrible spot, exposed to the cutting winds coming from the rue Férou and also occupied by a wine-shop with its captive clientele of thirsty choristers. And this part of the square interested him, offering as it did the sight of people holding onto their hats and almost getting blown over by the fierce gusts of wind, as they walked past the big omnibuses from la Villette, their sturdy russet chassis lining up along the pavement outside the church.

The square grew more lively, but without gaiety and without hubbub; the fiacres dozed at their ranks outside a five-centimes tavern and a beer hall; the huge yellow omnibuses from the Batignolles crisscrossed the roads, swinging to and fro, their routes intersected by the little green omnibus from the Pantheon and the pale two-horse coach from Auteuil; at noon, the seminarists would walk in procession, two by two, their eyes lowered, with the mechanical tread of automata, in a long, snaking line of black and white that led them from Saint-Sulpice to the seminary.

When the sun broke through, the square became charming: the asymmetric towers of the church took on a blond hue; the gold of the lettering sparkled all along the windows of the shops selling chasubles and holy ciboria, the huge signboard of a furniture remover's created a splash of even brighter and cruder colour, and, on the iron screen of a public urinal, a dyer's advertisement showed two scarlet hats, standing out starkly against a black background, which, in this district of church beadles and devout ladies, hinted at the splendours of religion, and the lofty dignities of the priestly vocation.

However, there was in this spectacle nothing novel for M. Folantin. How many times in his youth had he tramped across this square, so as to gaze at the old boar that used to be displayed by the Maison Bailly; how many times, in the evening, had he listened to the plaint of an open-air singer, near the fountain; how often had he sauntered round, on the days of the flower market, near the seminary?

He had long since exhausted the charm of this quiet spot; to savour it anew, he was now obliged to space out his visits, and walk through it only at rare intervals.

Thus, the Place Saint-Sulpice was no longer any help to him on a Sunday and he preferred the other days of the week, since he then had his office to go to and was less at a loose end; ah, there was no doubt about it: Sundays dragged on forever! On those mornings, he would have his breakfast a little later than usual, lingering on for ages at table, so as to give the caretaker time to clean his bedroom, and yet it was never tidied up when he went back; he tripped over the rolled-up carpets, and advanced through the clouds of dust raised by the broom. One! Two! – the caretaker pummelled the sheets into shape, laid the carpets back, and left, on the pretext that he didn't want to get in Monsieur's way.

M. Folantin picked up dust with his fingertips from every piece of furniture, tidied away his clothes that had been left in a heap on the armchair, gave a flick of a feather duster here and there and put some fresh cinders in his spittoon; then he counted the linen that the laundrywoman sometimes deigned to send back; he was assailed by such disgust at the sight of his mangled shirts that he stuffed them away in a drawer, without giving them a closer examination.

He could pick off the moments of the day reasonably well until four o'clock. He would read old letters from friends and relatives long since dead; he would leaf through a few of his books, pausing to savour a passage here and there, but around five o'clock he started to suffer; the time was drawing nigh when he would have to dress for dinner again; the very idea of having to clear out of his room took away his hunger and, on some Sundays, he didn't budge – or else, if he anticipated that his appetite might perk up belatedly, he would go down in his slippers and buy a couple of rolls, and some pâté or sardines. He always had a little chocolate and some wine put by in a cupboard and he would eat, happy to be at home, with plenty of room, able to stretch out and avoid, for once, the cramped space of a restaurant; the only problem was that his nights were bad; he would wake up with a start, suffering from hunger pangs, shivering and shaking; sometimes his insomnia would last an hour, and as the darkness gave new intensity to his gloomy ideas, he would chew over the same complaints as in the daytime, and end up regretting that he didn't have a partner. 'Marriage is out of the question at my age,' he would tell himself. 'Ah, if only I'd had a mistress in my youth, and kept her on, I'd be able to finish my days with her, and when I came home I would find my lamp lit and my dinner all ready. If I could see my time all over again, I'd live my life quite differently! I'd find a friendly person for my old age; there's no doubt about it, I've presumed too much on my own strength, I've come to the end of my tether.' And when morning broke, he got up on tottering legs, heavy-headed and unable to think straight.

It was in any case an unpleasant period; the winter was harsh, and the cold wind made his own place seem enviable in comparison with having to spend a deeply disagreeable time in small restaurants where the doors were constantly swinging open. And then, suddenly, M. Folantin found himself overwhelmed by a great hope. One morning, in the rue de Grenelle, he noticed that a new patisserie had set up. These words were gleaming in letters of copper on the windows: 'Meals delivered.'

It was a real revelation. Could it be that he was going to realise the dream he had nursed for so long, of having his dinners brought up to him? But then he came down to earth again, remembering his useless quests through the district in search of an establishment that did home deliveries.

It doesn't cost anything to ask, he finally told himself, and went in.

'Why, of course, Monsieur,' replied a young woman from the narrow space behind her counter, where she was hemmed in by cream-tarts and custard-pies. 'Nothing could be easier, seeing that you live only a stone's throw away. And what time would you like the food to be delivered?'

'Six o'clock,' said M. Folantin, trembling with excitement.

'Perfect!'

M. Folantin's face suddenly fell.

'Well now,' he said, stammering slightly, 'the thing is, I'd like some soup, a plate of meat and some veg; how much would it come to?'

The woman appeared to be absorbed in thought, murmuring, with her eyes raised to the sky, 'soup… meat… veg… You won't be having wine?'

'No, I've got some at home.'

'Well, Monsieur, in that case it would be two francs.'

M. Folantin's expression brightened up again. 'Fine,' he said, 'then that's settled; when can we start?'

'Whenever you like. This evening, if you want.'

'This very evening, Madame.' He bowed and the lady bowed in turn, her head coming down so low over the counter that her nose almost crushed the cream-tarts and dented the custard-pies.

Out in the street, M. Folantin came to a halt after a few steps. 'There we are! What a piece of luck!' he said to himself; then his rapture subsided. 'So long as the grub is merely edible. Dash it! I've put up with so many horrible meals in my poor life that I don't have any right to be picky. She's nice, that lady,' he continued; 'not all that pretty, but she does have expressive eyes; I hope she makes a success of it!' And as he trotted along, he made a wish for the prosperity of the patissière.

Finally, he did everything he could to ensure that the first evening went off without a hitch; he ordered six litres of wine from a grocer's, then, once he had arrived in his office, he drew up a short list of provisions he would buy:

Jam;

Cheese;

Biscuits;

Salt;

Pepper;

Mustard;

Vinegar;

Oil.

'I'll have my concierge bring my bread up every day; ah, Good Lord, if only it works out all right, I'll be saved!'

He longed for the end of the day; his haste to enjoy his solitary evening to the full made time seem to drag even more.

From time to time he would look at his watch.

His colleague, who had already been stupefied by the ecstatic expression on the face of M. Folantin as he dreamt of his cosy lodgings, smiled.

'Admit it! She's sitting there waiting for you,' he said.

'Who?' asked M. Folantin in the greatest astonishment.

'Come on, don't try to teach your grandmother to suck eggs. So tell me, all joking apart: is she a blonde or a brunette?'

'My dear friend!' replied M. Folantin, 'I can assure you that I really have other things to think about than women.'

'Yes, yes... I know: they all say the same. You old rascal! *You're* still game for it, I can see!'

'Come along, gentlemen, copy this, straight away; I need these two letters ready to be signed this evening,' said the chief as he came in and went out again.

'It's absurd, there are four dense pages,' grumbled M. Folantin; 'it'll be five o'clock before I finish. My God, what a nuisance!' he continued, turning to his colleague.

The latter sniggered, and said in a low voice, 'Good heavens, old chap! The administration can't think of everything, now, can it?'

He finished his task as well as he could, cursing all the while, then returned home by the shortest route, his arms laden with parcels and his pockets stuffed with bags; once he had shut his door behind him, he drew breath, put on his comfortable slippers, gave a quick wipe with a tea towel to the few knives and forks he possessed, cleaned his wineglasses and, finding neither the board nor the piece of sandstone he sharpened his knives on, stuck them into the soil of an old flowerpot and managed to give them a bit of a gleam.

'Phew!' he said, drawing the table up to the fire, 'I'm ready.' Six o'clock struck.

M. Folantin awaited the patissière's assistant with impatience and something of that feverish expectation which had prevented him, in his youth, from keeping still when a friend was late turning up at a meeting-place.

Finally, at quarter-past six, the doorbell rang and a young lad staggered in, nose first, dragged forward under the weight of a heavy tin-plate container in the shape of a bucket; M. Folantin helped to set out the plates on the table, and as soon as he was alone took the lids off. There was a tapioca soup, a piece of braised veal, and a cauliflower in white sauce.

'But it's not at all bad,' he said, tasting each of the dishes in turn, and he ate to his heart's content, drank a little more than usual, then fell into a gentle reverie, gazing round his room.

For several years he had been expressing the intention to decorate it, but he had told himself repeatedly, 'Oh, what's the point? I don't spend my whole life here; if later on I can arrange a different lifestyle for myself, I'll get round to sorting out my apartment.' But though he had bought nothing as yet, he already had his eye on several knick-knacks which he had spied as he roamed up and down the quays and the rue de Rennes.

The idea of adorning the glacial walls of his bedroom suddenly occurred to him as he was swigging down one last glass of wine. His indecision came to an end; he was determined to spend the few sous he had been saving up over the past few years with just this aim in mind, and he enjoyed a delightful evening, drawing up plans for a complete makeover of his humble abode. 'I'll get up early tomorrow,' he concluded, 'and I'll start off by taking a turn round the novelty shops and bric-à-brac sellers.'

His idleness was coming to an end; a new interest had slipped into his life; the preoccupation with discovering a few engravings or some pieces of faience that wouldn't be too much of a drain on his pocket kept him going, and after a day at the office, he would dash feverishly up from floor to floor of the Bon Marché or the Petit Saint-Thomas department stores, turning over masses of fabric, finding them too dark or too light, too narrow or too wide, rejecting the odd and ends and the various reduced items that the draper's assistants kept trying to palm off on him, and forcing them to bring out the merchandise they had been keeping in reserve. By pestering them and keeping them running around for hours on end, he finally got them to show him ready-made curtains and carpets that really caught his fancy.

After these purchases, and after fierce discussions with second-hand dealers and print sellers, he was left penniless; all his savings had been spent; but, like a child with new toys, M. Folantin examined his new acquisitions, turning them over again and again. He climbed up on chairs to fix the frames in place, and rearranged his books. 'It's nice staying at home,' he reflected; and it was quite true, his room was no longer recognisable. Instead of wallpaper torn by nails, it was decorated by wall-to-wall engravings of works by Ostade, Teniers, and all the painters of real life that he was such a fan of.[7] A real collector would have certainly shrugged in disdain at the sight of these unmounted prints, but M. Folantin was neither a connoisseur nor very wealthy; he mostly went for pictures showing the ordinary everyday life that he liked, and in any case he couldn't have cared less about the authenticity of his cheap prints, so long as the colours were effective and brightened up the walls.

'I should have changed my mahogany furniture too,' he said to himself as he considered his boat-shaped bed, his two Voltaire armchairs covered with damask that had gone brown, his dressing-table with its cracked marble, and his table with its reddish veneered wood. 'But it would have cost too much, and in any case, the curtains and the carpets are enough to give a new lease of life to this furniture which, like my old clothes, now perfectly suits my comings and goings and my little habits.'

So now he was really happy to come home, to put all the lights on, and sink into his armchair! The cold weather seemed to have been left outside, held at bay by the cosiness of his snug little den, and the falling snow, muffling all the street noises, added even more to his sense of well-being; in the silence of the evening, his dinner – as he toasted his feet by the fire, while the plates warmed in front of the grating, near the wine he put there to take the chill off it – was delicious; and the tedium of office life, and the sadness of his bachelor existence all melted away in this pacific quietude.

True enough, hardly a week had gone by and the patisserie food was starting to fall off. The inevitable tapioca was full of curds, and the bouillon was artificially made and full of chemical additives; the gravy on the meat stank of the sour Madeira of restaurants; all the dishes had an odd taste, an indefinable taste, a cross between a rather larded flour paste and stale, lukewarm vinegar. M. Folantin vigorously scattered pepper on his meat and added mustard to his gravy; 'come on, you can still force it down!' he said, 'the essential thing is to get used to this kind of grub!'

But the quality of the dishes was not going to remain on the level of the merely mediocre and, little by little, the decline accelerated, aggravated by the constant lateness of the patissière's boy. He would arrive at seven o'clock, covered with snow, his plate-warmer all cold; he had two black eyes, and there were scratches all down his cheeks. M. Folantin could have no doubt about it; the boy was putting his container down next to a bollard and getting involved in regular fights with kids of his own age. He mildly said as much to the boy, who started snivelling, swore black was white, called Heaven to witness and insisted, hand on heart, that this was completely untrue; but he just went on even worse than before; and M. Folantin said nothing, moved by pity, and not daring to complain to the patissière, for fear of damaging the lad's future prospects.

For another month he valiantly put up with all these discomfitures; and yet his heart sank when he had to fish out the meat that had fallen to the bottom of the tinplate container, for there were days when a tempest seemed to have been unleashed on the contents; everything was upside down, and the white sauce had got mixed up with the tapioca, which had little pieces of hot coal embedded in it.

There was, fortunately, a period of respite: the patissière's boy had been given the sack, doubtless as a result of the complaints of people less indulgent than M. Folantin. His successor was a tall thin vacant-looking youth, a sort of simpleton to judge by his appearance, pasty-faced and with big red hands. This one at least was punctual, arriving at six on the dot, but he was disgustingly dirty; he was dressed in kitchen rags stiff with grease and filth, his cheeks were smeared with flour and soot and he never wiped his nose, so that two green furrows trickled down to the sides of his mouth.

M. Folantin took energetic measures to parry this new blow of fate; he gave up on the sauces and dirty dishes; he transferred the meat to one of his own plates, scraped it dry, cleaned it, and ate it with plenty of salt.

Despite his resignation, the moment came when certain dishes made him feel sick. Now he found himself sampling all the forcemeat recipes that had gone wrong, all the pastries that had been burnt or spoilt by cinders from the stove; he kept fishing out lumps of old piecrusts out of every dish; emboldened by his benevolence, the patissière was laying aside all sense of shame and decency and sending him all the leftovers from her kitchen.

'She's poisoning me!' murmured M. Folantin as he passed the shop of the patissière, whom he no longer thought of as being so nice; and he looked at her askance, having lost all desire to wish her prosperity in her business.

And he resorted to hard-boiled eggs. He bought some every day, fearing that his dinner that evening would yet again prove inedible. And every day he ate huge quantities of salad; but the eggs were putrid, as the fruit-and-vegetable seller sold him the least fresh eggs in her shop, viewing him as someone who wouldn't be able to tell the difference.

'Let's try and make it through to the spring,' said M. Folantin to himself to buck up his morale; but from week to week his energy started to flag, just as his body, deplorably undernourished, cried famine. His gaiety subsided; his private life grew more dismal; the procession of anguished feelings that had previously dogged him again hemmed him in on every side. 'If only I had something to feel passionate about; if only I liked women, or my office, if only I enjoyed cafés, dominoes, or cards, I could have my meals out,' he ruminated, 'and I would never stay at home. But oh dear me! Nothing is any fun, nothing interests me; and then my digestion is up the spout! Ah, I shouldn't complain, but people who can afford to buy food but can't eat because they have no appetite are just as much to be pitied as the wretches who haven't a penny to appease their hunger!'

4

One evening, as he was picking at eggs that smelt of pooh, the concierge presented him with an invitation as follows:

†

Monsieur,

The nuns of the Company of St Agatha most humbly beg you to commend to God in your prayers and at the Holy Sacrifice of the Mass, the soul of their dear sister Ursule-Aurélie Bougeard, nun and chorister, who passed away on 7th September 1880, in the sixty-second year of her age and the thirty-fifth of her religious profession, consoled by the Sacraments of Our Holy Mother Church.

De profundis!

Sweet heart of Mary, be my salvation.

(300 days indulgence.)

She was a cousin of his whom he had briefly met once or twice, long ago, in his youth; ever since, for twenty years, he had hardly spared her a thought, and yet the death of this woman affected him deeply; she was his last relative and he felt even more alone now that she had passed away, in some distant provincial place. He envied her calm and silent life and he longed for the faith that he had lost. What a profession was prayer, what a pastime was confession, what an outlet religious practices created for you! In the evenings you go to church and become absorbed in profound contemplation, and the miseries of life count for little; then your Sundays go by bit by bit in the long services, amid the languorous canticles and vespers, for spleen has no hold over pious souls.

'Yes, but why is this consoling religion only made for the poor in spirit? Why has the Church wanted to erect the most absurd beliefs into dogmas? It's true that if you had faith... yes, but I've lost mine...' and in any case, the bigotry of the clergy revolted him. 'And yet,' he continued, 'religion alone could heal the wound that afflicts me. And in any case, it's wrong to demonstrate to the faithful how foolish their devotions really are, for people are happy when they can accept as a temporary trial all the vexations and afflictions of this present life. Ah! Aunt Ursule must have died without any regrets, convinced that infinite joys were about to unfold before her eyes!'

He thought about her, and tried to recall the features of her face, but his memory had preserved no trace of her; so, to draw a little nearer to her, to participate to some degree in the life she had led, he reread the mysterious and insightful chapter in *Les Misérables* devoted to the Petit-Picpus convent.

'Good Lord! It's a high price to pay for the unlikely happiness of a future life,' he said to himself. The convent struck him as a prison, a place of desolation and terror. 'No, no! None of that! I don't envy Aunt Ursule's fate any more; but all the same, the unhappiness of one person doesn't make up for the unhappiness of another, and meanwhile the pigswill from the patisserie is becoming inedible.'

Two days later he received another blow, like a cold shower full on his cranium.

To vary his diet a bit from the dinners composed of salad and dessert, he went back to a restaurant; there was no one there, but the service was slow and the wine had a whiff of benzine.

'At any rate, you don't get trampled in the rush, and that's something,' M. Folantin told himself as he tried to cheer himself up.

The door half opened and a draught blew up his back; he heard a great rustle of skirts and a shadow fell across his table. There was a woman standing in front of him, shifting the chair on the bars of which he had been resting his feet. She sat down, and placed her hat veil and her gloves next to her glass.

'Devil take her,' he grumbled, 'she has all those empty tables to choose from, and she has to come and sit down at mine!'

Mechanically, he looked up from the plate he had been fixing with his stare, and could not refrain from inspecting his neighbour. She had the face of a little monkey, a crumpled expression with a rather big mouth spread beneath a snub nose, and tiny little black moustaches at the corners of her lips; despite her playful appearance she still conveyed to him an impression of politeness and reserve.

From time to time she darted a quick glance at him and, in a very gentle voice, asked him to pass her the water jug or the bread. In spite of his shyness, M. Folantin was obliged to answer a few questions she put to him; little by little they struck up a conversation and, by the time they reached the dessert, they were deploring, not knowing what else to say, the bitter wind that was blowing outside and freezing their legs.

'It's weather like this that makes you feel it would be nice not to have to sleep alone,' said the woman, dreamily.

This remark completely flummoxed M. Folantin, who felt it best not to reply.

'Don't you think so, Monsieur?' she continued.

'Good Lord!... Mademoiselle...' And like a coward throwing down his weapons so as not to have to fight his adversary, M. Folantin confessed his chaste life, his few wants, his relief at being free of carnal desire.

'Are you sure?' she said, looking him straight in the eye.

He was troubled, especially as the bust she was advancing towards him gave out the aroma of new-mown hay and amber.

'I'm not twenty any more and, to be honest, I don't have any hopes – if indeed I ever did. I'm too old for that sort of thing.' And he pointed to his bald head, his leaden complexion, his clothes that were in no identifiable fashion.

'Come off it. You're joking, you're making yourself out to be older than you are.' And she added that she didn't like young men, she preferred mature men, since they know how to handle a woman.

'Of course... of course...' stammered M. Folantin, and asked for the bill; the woman didn't take out her purse, and he realised that it was up to him to pick up the tab. He paid the sardonic waiter for the two meals and was getting ready to wish the woman good day, at the door, when she calmly took his arm.

'So are you going to take me with you, Monsieur?'

He tried to find an excuse, find some way round this dire peril, but he became confused and his self-control wilted under the gaze of the woman whose perfumery rose headily to his brain.

'I can't,' he finally replied, 'we're not allowed to take women back to the place where I live.'

'In that case you can come to my place.' And she pressed herself against him, starting to coax and wheedle, claiming that she had a nice fire burning in her room. Then, seeing the gloomy expression on M. Folantin's face, she sighed. 'So, don't you like me?'

'Oh yes, Madame... of course I do... but one can find a woman charming, and still not...'

She started to laugh. 'What a funny fellow!' she said, and kissed him.

M. Folantin was deeply embarrassed by this kiss in the open street; he sensed how grotesque it must seem, an old man with a limp, being coddled in public by a girl. He tried to pull away and escape from these caresses, fearing at the same time that he would, if he tried to flee, cause a ridiculous scene which would bring everyone running up to stare.

'It's here,' she said, and pushed him gently along, marching behind him and cutting off his retreat. He climbed up to the third floor and, contrary to the woman's assertions, found no fire lit in her place.

He looked sheepishly at the room, whose walls seemed to be trembling in the flickering light of a candle; it was a room with blue-upholstered furniture, and a sofa with a striped pattern. A muddy boot was lying around under a chair and there was a pair of kitchen tongs opposite it under the table; here and there, the adverts of semolina makers, and chaste coloured prints representing babies smeared with soup, had been pinned to the walls; the bottom of a cooking-pot peeped out from the grate that had not been properly closed, and on the fake marble shelf above, there were scattered, next to an alarm clock and a half-empty glass, some pomade wrapped in a playing-card, shreds of tobacco, and strands of hair in a piece of newspaper.

'Well, make yourself at home,' said the woman, and when he refused to remove his clothes, she took hold of the sleeves of his overcoat and seized his hat.

'J.F. – I bet you're called Jules,' she said, looking at the letters on the lining.

He confessed that his name was Jean.

'That's not such a bad name. Well now!' – and she forced him to sit on a sofa, and hopped onto his lap.

'Tell me, darling, what are you going to give me so I can buy some nice new gloves?'

M. Folantin reluctantly extracted a hundred-sous coin from his pocket and she deftly spirited it away.

'Go on, you can give me another one like that, I'll take my clothes off; you'll see, I can be really nice.'

M. Folantin yielded, declaring all the same that he would prefer it if she wasn't naked, and then she kissed him so skilfully that a breath of youthful vigour returned to him, he forgot his resolutions and lost his head; then, at one point, as he was hesitating in his attentions and yet starting to hurry things along, she said, 'Don't bother about me... don't bother about me... just look after yourself.'

M. Folantin slowly made his way down from the whore's room, filled with profound nausea; and, as he made his way back to his lodgings, he took in at a glance the desolate horizon of his life; he realised the futility of changing direction, the sterility of all enthusiasm and all effort; 'You have to let yourself go with the flow; Schopenhauer is right,' he told himself, '"Man's life swings like a pendulum between pain and boredom." So there's no point in trying to speed up or slow down the rhythm of its swings; all we can do is fold our arms and try to get to sleep; how I regret trying to live the way I used to, wanting to go to the theatre, to smoke a decent cigar, to swallow tonics and go after a woman; how I regret leaving one bad restaurant to go gallivanting off to another that was no better, and all this to end up eating filthy vol-au-vents from a patisserie!'

Mulling over these thoughts, he had arrived outside his lodgings. 'Ah, I've got no matches,' he thought, rummaging in his pockets as he climbed the stairs; he pushed the door open into his room, a cold chill froze his face and, feeling his way forward in the dark, he sighed: 'The easiest thing is to go back to the old greasy spoon, and return tomorrow to the horrid fold. So it's true: when you're penniless, there's no hope of ever getting the best; only the worst happens.'

M. Bougran's Retirement

1

M. Bougran gazed in consternation at the imprecise flower pattern on the carpet.

'Yes,' continued the chief clerk, M. Devin, in a benevolent tone, 'yes, my dear colleague, I defended you to the hilt, I tried to get the personnel office to review its decision, but my efforts failed; as from next month you are being retired, due to infirmities resulting from the exercise of your functions.'

'But I don't have any infirmities, I'm perfectly healthy!'

'No doubt, but a man like you doesn't need me to tell you anything about the legislation on this matter; the law of 9th June 1853 on civil pensions permits, as you well know... this interpretation; the decree of 9th November of the same year, which lays down the terms within the service for the execution of the said law, states in one of its articles...'

'Article 30,' sighed M. Bougran.

'Just as I was about to say... it states that civil servants can be prematurely retired as a result of psychological infirmity, undetectable by men of the medical art.'

M. Bougran had stopped listening. With the gaze of a stunned animal his eyes wandered round the chief clerk's study, which he usually entered on tiptoe, respectfully, as if he were entering a chapel. This dry, cold, but familiar room, suddenly struck him as sullen and bloated, hostile, with its green matt wallpaper with velvet stripes, its glass-fronted bookshelves painted in oak and full of legal documents, 'collections of administrative acts', all preserved in those bindings special to ministries – bindings in mottled calfskin, with wooden boards and yellow edges – its mantelpiece adorned with a massive clock, two Empire candlesticks, its horsehair sofa, its carpet with roses looking like cabbages, its mahogany table laden with bundles of paper and books, on which was perched a rosette-shaped bell, studded with almond-shaped decorations, to summon people with, its armchairs with their wheezy springs, its office chair with its cane worn down at the arms by long use into a half-moon shape.

Bored with the interview, M. Devin rose and went to stand with his back to the fire, whose ashes he fanned with the tails of his frock-coat.

M. Bougran came back to his senses and very faintly asked, 'Have they chosen my successor, so that I can bring him up to date before I leave?'

'Not as far as I know; so I'll be obliged if you will continue in post until further notice.'

And to hasten M. Bougran's departure, M. Devin left the mantelpiece and advanced slowly towards his employee, who retreated towards the door; there, M. Devin assured him of his deep regret and his profound esteem.

M. Bougran returned to his own office and sank down, like a broken man, on a chair. Then he felt as if he were being suffocated; he put on his hat and went out to get a breath of fresh air. He walked through the streets and, without even knowing where he was, he finally ended up on a bench in a small square.

So it was true; he had been retired at the age of fifty! He, who had been such a devoted employee that he had even sacrificed his Sundays and his holidays so that the work he was responsible for would not suffer any delay. And this was all the gratitude he got for his zeal! He felt a momentary anger, and dreamt of appealing to the Council of State, then, coming down to earth, he told himself, 'I'll lose my case and it'll cost me dear.' Slowly and calmly he mentally went through all the articles of that law; he examined every trail through that dense prose, tested the gangways thrown across from article to article; at first sight, these paths seemed quite safe, well lit and straight; then, little by little, they would ramify, leading to shadowy turnings, dark dead-ends where you suddenly fell flat on your face.

'Yes, the 1853 legislator has laid traps all over the place in this indulgent text. He has foreseen everything,' concluded M. Bougran, 'hence the case of "suppression of job" which is one of those most frequently used to get rid of people; you suppress the job held by the man in question, then you re-establish it a few days later under a new description, and lo and behold, Bob's your uncle! There are always the physical infirmities contracted in the exercise of your functions and verified by the doctors, who are quick to do what is asked of them; and then there is – and basically this is the simplest method – so-called psychological infirmity, for which there's no need to resort to any practitioner, since a simple report, signed by your Director and approved by the Personnel Manager, is enough.

'This is the most humiliating system. To have them judging you senile! It's too much!' groaned M. Bougran.

Then he started to reflect. The minister doubtless had some protégé he needed to find a job for, since there were fewer and fewer employees who really had a right to take retirement. For years there had been swingeing cutbacks in the offices, replacing the older staff, of which he was one of the last remnants, with new blood. And M. Bougran nodded.

'In my time,' he said, 'we were conscientious and full of enthusiasm; now all these little youngsters, recruited from Heaven knows where, have none of the faith we had. They don't go right to the bottom of any business, they don't study any text in detail. All they can think of is escaping from the office, so they bodge their work, and can't be bothered to learn the language of administration that the older generation manipulated so adroitly; they all write as if they were just writing personal letters! Even the chief clerks, enlisted for the most part from outside, the flotsam and jetsam of whole series of ministers fallen from power, no longer have that bearing at once friendly and haughty which used to distinguish them from ordinary folk'; and forgetting his own misadventure, in a respectful vision he dwelt on the image of one of his former chief clerks, M. Desrots des Bois, trussed up in his frock-coat, his buttonhole concealed by an enormous red disc like the 'Stop!' sign for trains, the temples of his bald head encircled by fluffy down like a chick's, descending the stairs straight-backed, not turning to look at anyone, a portfolio under his arm, en route to see the director.

Every head bowed as he passed. The employees could well believe that this man's importance redounded on them and they derived a greater sense of self-esteem from it.

At that time, everything was done in due form, and the nuances that had now vanished still existed. In administrative letters, there were different terms used to refer to the petitioners: the full 'Monsieur Dupont', for a person who held an honourable rank in society, plain 'Dupont' for a less distinguished man, and 'a certain Dupont' for workers and convicts. And what ingenious devices they used to vary the vocabulary and avoid having to repeat the same words! They would designate the petitioner as 'the postulant', then 'the suppliant', then 'the plaintiff', then 'the applicant'. The prefect would become, in another part of the sentence, 'that high functionary'; the person whose name was the reason for the letter would change into 'this individual', or 'the abovementioned', or 'the aforesaid'; in referring to itself, the service would sometimes describe itself as 'central' and sometimes as 'superior'; it made lavish use of synonyms, and added, as the envoi to a letter, phrases such as 'find attached, enclosed, herewith'. Protocols ran on and on; the signing-off formulae at the end of letters could take infinitely varying forms, all precisely calculated, on a scale which demanded from the office pianists a rare talent for fingering. In one letter, addressed to the pinnacle of the hierarchy, it was the assurance 'of our deepest and most humble respect', then as the degree of respect diminished, for men without ministerial rank, it became 'our humble respect', 'our deep respect', 'our great respect', 'our cordial respect', ending up as respect full stop, a respect which cancelled itself out, representing as it did the height of contempt.

Which employee now knew how to manipulate that delicate keyboard to strike the right note at the end of letters, choosing those deferential terms that were sometimes so difficult to determine when it was a matter of replying to people whose status hadn't been foreseen by the imperfectly laid-down dogmas of the protocols! Ah, the copying clerks had lost all sense for the right turn of phrase, and were ignorant of the skilful game of measuring respect out drop by drop! And what did it matter, after all, since for years everything had been falling apart, relapsing into chaos. The time of democratic abominations had come and the title of 'Excellency' that ministers had once exchanged with each other had disappeared. They wrote from one ministry to another on an equal footing, like shopkeepers or ordinary middle-class folk. Even the favours, those silk ribbons in blue, green or tricolour, which used to tie together letters when they consisted of more than two pages, had been replaced by pink string, at five sous a ball!

How commonplace everything had become! What a come-down! 'I never felt at home in that environment devoid of any real dignity or bearing, but... but... that's not the same as actually wanting to leave...' And with a sigh, M. Bougran returned to his own situation and turned his thoughts to his own plight.

In his head he totted up the proportional pension he would be able to claim: eighteen hundred francs at most; with the small fixed income his father had given him, there would be just enough to live on. 'It's true,' he said to himself, 'that my old servant Eulalie and I get by on nothing.'

But much more of a worry than the question of personal resources was the question of how he would manage to kill the time. How could he break away overnight from the habit of being shut up in the same old office room, for identical hours each day, and participating in the customary exchange of conversation each morning with his colleagues? True, the talk had not been very varied; it generally concerned the greater or lesser degree of promotion to be expected at the end of the year, as the clerks tried to work out who was due for retirement, and even tried to guess who might die, or imagined illusory perks, deviating from these fascinating subjects only in order to launch out into interminable reflections on the events related in the newspaper. But even this lack of novelty was in such perfect harmony with the monotony of the faces, the flatness of the jokes, and, indeed, the uniformity of the office rooms!

Then there had been, after all, some interesting discussions in the office of the chief clerk or his deputy, on the best way of swinging this or that piece of business. What now would replace those juridical jousts, those apparent disputes, those cheerful agreements, those welcome quarrels? How could he find anything entertaining enough to make him forget a profession that pierced you to the marrow, possessed you entirely, to the very depths of your being?

And M. Bougran shook his head in despair, telling himself, 'I'm alone, a bachelor, without family, friends or acquaintances; I have no talent to take up any job other than the one that has kept me busy for the past twenty years. I'm too old to start out on a new life.' This realisation terrified him.

'Well,' he resumed as he rose to his feet, 'I've still got to go back to my office!' His legs were unsteady. 'I don't feel very well; what if I went and had a lie-down?' But he forced himself to walk, resolved to die with harness on his back. He made his way to the ministry, and returned to his office.

There he really and truly almost fainted away. He looked around in dismay, tears in his eyes, at this shell which had protected him for so many years – while his colleagues softly entered in single file.

They had been awaiting his return and their condolences varied with the expression on their faces. The assistant clerk, a tall gangling fellow with the head of a stork, across whose cranium a few colourless hairs straggled, shook him fervently by the hand, without uttering a word; his demeanour was that of someone consoling the family of a dead man, on leaving church while the bier is waiting outside, after the absolution. The copying clerks wagged their heads, demonstrating their official sympathy by repeated bows.

The clerks who drafted the letters, who, being his colleagues, knew him better, tried to think of a few words of comfort.

'Come now, you have to make the best of a bad job – and then, old chap, just think that when it comes down to it, you have neither wife, not children, you could have been retired in much more difficult circumstances, if you'd had a daughter to marry off, for instance – as I do. So you can count yourself as lucky as anyone can be in a similar situation.'

'It's only right to look on the bright side, whatever happens,' said another. 'You're going to be free to take walks, you can live off your income and laze in the sunshine.'

'And you can go and live in the countryside – you'll be in clover!' added a third.

M. Bougran mildly pointed out that he had been born in Paris, that he knew nobody out in the provinces, that he didn't feel he had the strength to go into exile in some hole or other just so as to save money; all of them continued, nonetheless, to demonstrate to him that, all things considered, he wasn't so very badly off.

And as none of them was of an age to feel threatened by a similar fate, they exhibited a genuine resignation, almost waxing indignant at the sadness shown by M. Bougran.

The finest example of real sympathy and authentic regret was Baptiste, the office boy, Bougran's main assistant. With an air of unctuous consternation, he offered to carry M. Bougran's odds and ends home for him – his old overcoat, his pens, pencils, etc., all his office possessions – intimating that this would be the last time M. Bougran would have the opportunity of giving him a fat tip.

'Come now, gentlemen,' said the chief clerk as he entered the office room. 'The Director wants the portfolio ready for five o'clock.'

They all went back to their desks; and, whinnying like an old horse, M. Bougran settled down to work, his mind entirely occupied by the task in hand, hurrying to make up for the time he had wasted indulging in gloomy daydreams on the bench.

2

The first days were quite awful. Waking at the same time as before, he asked himself what was the point of getting up, continued to lounge in bed, quite contrary to his normal habits, started to feel cold, yawned, and finally got dressed. But Good Lord, what was he to do to fill his time? On mature reflection, he decided to go for a walk and take a stroll round the Luxembourg Gardens, which were not far from the rue de Vaugirard where he lived.

But those immaculately manicured lawns, without a trace of earth or water, that looked as if they were freshly repainted and varnished each morning as soon as the sun rose; those flowers raised erect as if newly blossoming on their wiry stalks; those trees with all the girth of reeds, that whole artificial landscape, planted with ridiculous statues – none of this cheered him. He went to take refuge at the far end of the garden, in the former seed-bed over which the constructions of the Ecole de Pharmacie and the Lycée Louis-le-Grand cast their solemn shadows. The verdure here was just as glossily kept and emaciated as elsewhere. The lawns spread out their grass, cropped short and green, the little trees nodded the bored plumes of their heads, but the torture inflicted on the fruit trees, in certain of the flower-beds, made him halt. These trees no longer had the shape of trees. They were made to extend their branches along wooden laths, or to crawl along wires laid out on the ground; their limbs were twisted into odd shapes as soon as they were born. In this way, acrobatical vegetation was produced, with trunks that bent every which way, as flexible as if they had been made of rubber. They ran along, snaking like adders, rose like conical baskets, mimicked beehives, pyramids, fan shapes, vases of flowers, or a clown's tuft of hair. This garden was a real torture chamber for trees and shrubs; here, with the help of racks, and boots of wickerwork or cast iron, straw contraptions, and orthopaedic corsets, gardeners with hernias tried, not so much to straighten the curved and twisted limbs as do the bandage makers of humanity, but to do the precise opposite, forcing them into strange shapes, dislocating them and twisting them, in accordance with some putative Japanese ideal designed to produce monsters!

But when he had spent some time admiring this way of murdering trees on the pretext of extorting better fruit from them, he wandered up and down, at a loose end, without having even realised that this vegetable-garden surgery represented the most perfect symbol of the civil service that he had known and worked in for years. In office life, as in the Luxembourg Gardens, they went out of their way to take simple things to bits and pieces; they took some legal administrative text whose meaning was clear and precise, and immediately, with the help of turbid and circular arguments, unprecedented precedents, and jurisprudential quibbles going back to the Messidors and Ventôses of Revolutionary times,[8] they turned this text into a hopeless muddle, a contorted piece of literature grimacing like an ape, which produced decisions that were the complete opposite of the ones that could have been anticipated.

Then he made his way back up to the terrace of the Luxembourg, where the trees seem less young, less freshly dusted, more true to life. And he walked along between the garden chairs, watching the children make mud pies in the sand with their little buckets, while their mothers enjoyed a natter, shoulder to shoulder, energetically swapping ideas on the best way to cook veal and how to use the leftovers for the next day's lunch.

And, feeling worn out, he returned home, climbed the stairs, yawning, and received a scolding from his maid Eulalie, who complained that he was turning into a real 'pain in the neck' if he imagined he could come and 'troll around' in her kitchen.

Soon, insomnia was added to his woes; torn away from its habits, transported into an atmosphere of oppressive sloth, his body no longer functioned properly; his appetite had fled; his nights which had previously been so peaceful under the blankets became restless and filled with dark ideas, while, in the black silence, one by one, the hours chimed in the distance.

He tried spending the days reading, when it rained, and then, worn out by his insomnia, he fell asleep; and the night that followed these periods of slumber became even longer, even more wakeful. Even when the weather turned nasty, he found he still had to go for a walk, to tire his legs out, and he fetched up in the museums – but not a single painting aroused his interest; he did not recognise a single canvas or a single great artist, and he ambled slowly along, his hands behind his back, from frame to frame, his thoughts occupied by the attendants who were drowsing on their chairs, totting up the pension that they too, as state functionaries, could one day count on.

Tired of colours and white statues, he went for a stroll through the Parisian passages, but he was quickly sent packing; he was observed; the words 'informer', 'copper's nark', 'spy' were heard. Shamefaced he fled back out into the downpour and rushed to take refuge in his home.

And, more poignant than ever, the memory of his office obsessed him. Seen from afar, the ministry appeared to him as a real paradise. He had quite forgotten the iniquities he had endured, his post as under-chief-clerk nabbed by an outsider who had entered the service on the coat-tails of a minister, the irritations of a job that was both mechanical and stressful; the darker side of this existence spent polishing your chair with the seat of your pants had evaporated; all that was left was the vision of a nice sedentary life, cosy and warm, made cheery by the conversation of his colleagues, by their awful puns and their third-rate practical jokes.

'There's nothing for it: I must think of something to do,' said M. Bougran to himself, glumly. For a few hours he imagined that he could look for a new job that would keep him busy and even bring in a bit of money; but, even if there were some shopkeeper prepared to take on a man of his age, he would then have to slave away, morning, noon, and night, and he would have only a derisory wage since he wasn't up to doing a real job, in a profession whose secrets and tricks-of-the-trade he was ignorant of.

And it would be such a come-down in the world! – For, like many government employees, M. Bougran considered himself to be a member of a superior caste, and he despised the people who worked in commerce and banking. He even ranged his peers into hierarchies, judging a ministry employee superior to the employee of a prefecture, just as the latter was, in his eyes, of a higher rank than the petty clerk employed in a town hall.

So, what could he turn to? What was he to do? And this nagging question remained unanswered.

For want of anything better, he went back to his office on the pretext of seeing his colleagues, but he was received by them in the way that people who are no longer part of the group are always received – coldly. They enquired indifferently after his health; a few of them pretended to envy him, vaunted the freedom he enjoyed, the strolls he must be able to indulge in.

M. Bougran smiled, heavy-hearted. One final blow was accidentally inflicted on him. He allowed himself to be dragged over to his old office room; he saw the employee who had replaced him, a complete youngster! He was filled with rage against this successor, who had changed the appearance of the room that M. Bougran loved, shifting the desk, pushing the chairs over into another corner, filing the folders away in different pigeon-holes; the inkpot was now on the left, and the pen holder on the right!

He left, feeling completely despondent.

On the way home, suddenly, an idea sprang up and grew in his mind. 'Ah!' he thought, 'Perhaps I'm saved!' And such was his joy that, back home that evening, he ate with a hearty appetite, slept like a log, and awoke, in the best of humour, at first light.

3

The plan that had put him in such a good mood was easy to carry out. At first, M. Bougran did the rounds of the wallpaper shops, purchased several rolls of a horrible chicory- and milk-coloured paper that he hung on the walls of the smallest room in his apartment; then he bought a desk in black-painted pinewood, with a row of compartments on top; a little table on which he placed a chipped basin and a piece of marshmallow soap in an old glass, a semicircular cane armchair, and two chairs. He had his walls set up with pigeon-holes in white wood, that he filled with green folders with copper clasps, pinned a calendar over the mantelpiece from which he had first removed the mirror and piled boxes of slips on the shelf, slung a doormat on the floor and a waste-paper basket under his desk, and, stepping back, exclaimed in delight: 'That's it! I'm there!'

On his desk, he set out, methodically, the whole row of his pen holders and pencils – cork pen holders in the shape of a sledgehammer, copper-armoured pen holders sheathed in rosewood that were good to chew on, and black, blue and red pencils for the annotations and cross-references. Then he arranged, just as in bygone days, a porcelain inkwell, encircled with sponges, to the right of his desk blotter, a small bowl full of wood shavings on the left; opposite, a container with a grotesque face, its green velvet lid, bristling with pins, concealing rubber stamps and pink string. Dossiers of yellowish paper were scattered about pretty much everywhere; over the pigeon-holes were ranged the necessary tomes: Bloch's *Dictionary of Administration*, the *Civil Code*, the legal reference works, Bécquet and Blanche. He found himself back in front of his old desk in his old office room, without having budged an inch.

He sat down, radiant, and from that moment on he relived the halcyon days of yore. Every morning he would leave his home, just as he used to, and stepping out like a man eager to arrive on time he would stride down the boulevard Saint-Germain, stopping halfway towards his former office, then retrace his steps, return home, taking out his watch to check the time as he climbed the stairs, and he would lift the cardboard lid of his inkwell, remove his cuffs, replace them with cuffs in thick Manila paper, of the kind used to cover the dossiers, change his own suit of clothes for the old frock coat he used to wear at the ministry, and *voilà*! He could get down to work!

He would make up questions to be decided, address petitions to himself, reply to them, keep what is called a 'register' by writing in a big thick book the date of arrivals and departures. And, once his office hours came to an end, he would take an hour-long stroll, just as in bygone days, through the streets, before returning home for dinner.

He had the good fortune, at first, to dream up a problem of the kind he had enjoyed solving in bygone days, but one more muddled, more chimerical, more outlandishly inane. He slogged long and hard over it, searched through the decisions of the Council of State and the Court of Appeal for the judgements that can be used, as you like, to defend or support this case or that. Happy to wade through the baroque complexities of the law, trying to find ridiculous jurisprudential details that he could bend this way and that to fit his thesis, he sweated over his papers, starting his minutes or his drafts several times over again from scratch, correcting them in the margin he had left blank, just as his chief clerk had done in former times, never managing, in spite of all this, to satisfy himself, gnawing his pen holder, striking his brow, suffocating, and opening the window for a breath of fresh air.

He lived like this for a month; then he was seized by a sense of malaise. He would work until five o'clock, but he felt exhausted, discontented, distracted, incapable of seeing things in perspective, his head filled by his dossiers. By now, he was aware of the make-believe he had got caught up in; he had indeed restored the ambience of his former office, of the very room he had worked in. He left the door and window shut, if need be, so it would retain that smell of dust and dried ink that emanates from the rooms in the ministries – but the noise, the conversation, the comings and goings of his colleagues were all missing. Not a soul to talk to. This solitary office was not, when all was said and done, a real office. It was no use his having resumed all his old habits, it just wasn't the same. – Ah! he would have given a great deal to have been able to ring, so as to see the office boy come in and have a chat for a few minutes.

And then… and then… other holes were starting to open up in the artificial soil of this slack life; in the morning, as he went through the letters he had sent himself the day before, he knew what the envelopes contained; he recognised his own writing, the format of the envelope in which he had enclosed this piece of business or that, and this destroyed his every illusion! He would at least have needed there to be another person who wrote the address and used envelopes that he couldn't recognise!

He was overwhelmed by discouragement; he grew so bored that he allowed himself to take a few days off, and wandered through the streets.

'Monsieur is looking peaky,' said Eulalie when she looked at her master. And, her hands in her apron pockets, she added, 'I really can't understand anyone working so hard when it doesn't bring any money in!'

He sighed and, when she left, contemplated his face in the mirror. Still, it was true that he looked peaky: and how old he had grown! His eyes, a startled and mournful blue, always opened wide, in a fixed stare, were surrounded by wrinkles and his bushy eyebrows were turning white. His cranium was going bald, his side-whiskers were all grey, even his clean-shaven mouth had drooped, and was outshone by his prominent chin; his whole podgy little body was sagging, his shoulders stooping, his clothes seemed too big for him now, and looked much shabbier. He saw himself ruined, decrepit, crushed by the weight of the fifty years that he had borne so cheerfully as long as he was working in a real office.

'Monsieur ought to take a purgative,' Eulalie kept saying each time she saw him. 'Monsieur is bored; why doesn't he go fishing? He could bring us back a nice fish to fry from the Seine, it would be a change for him.'

M. Bougran gently shook his head, and went out.

One day, a chance stroll led him, without his even noticing, to the Jardin des Plantes, and his gaze was suddenly drawn by an arm waving on the edge of his line of vision. He stopped, pulled himself together, and saw one of his former office assistants greeting him.

He had a moment's illumination; almost a shout of joy.

'Huriot,' he said. The other turned round, lifted his cap, and shouldered the pipe he was holding.

'Well now, old friend, what's become of you, then?'

'Oh, nothing, M. Bougran, I'm doing odd jobs here and there to save up a few more pennies for my pension; but, saving your presence, I'm just bumming around, as I'm not much use for anything these days, ever since my legs have stopped working!'

'Listen, Huriot, do you still have one of the uniforms you used to wear in the ministry?'

'Oh yes, Monsieur, I've got an old one I use at home so I can save my best clothes for when I go out.'

'Ah!'

M. Bougran was rapt in a delightful daydream: take him into

his service at home, in his office uniform! Every quarter of an hour he would come into his room, bringing papers, just as before. And then he'd be able to take care of the dispatches, writing the addresses on the envelopes. It would perhaps be like *real* office life, at long last!

'Listen, my boy, I've got something to tell you,' M. Bougran went on. 'I'll pay you fifty francs a month to come to my place, exactly like the office – *exactly*, do you understand? You won't have all those stairs to go up and come down; but you can go and shave off your beard and grow sideburns like you used to, and wear your uniform again. Does that grab your fancy?'

'Does it half!' – And, as he hesitated, he screwed up his eyes. 'So, are you going to set up your own company, a bank or something, M. Bougran?'

'No, it's something else: I'll explain when the time comes; meanwhile, here's my address. Make whatever arrangements you need to, but turn up at my place tomorrow, and you can start work.'

And he left him and trotted back home, feeling rejuvenated.

'Good! That's what Monsieur ought to look like every day,' said Eulalie, observing him, and wondering what event had managed to rear its head into this monotonous life.

He needed to pour out his heart, to express his joy, to talk. He told his maid the story of his encounter, then he stood there, anxious and mute as she gazed sternly at him.

'So this gentleman is going to come here to do nothing but eat up your funds, just like that!' she said, dryly.

'No, no, Eulalie, he'll have his work to do, and in any case he's a good chap, an old civil servant who knows his job thoroughly.'

'That's not much use! Look, I bet that for fifty francs he'll sit there twiddling his thumbs while I get only forty francs a month – and *I* do the housework and the cooking, and take good care of you! – It's too much, it really is! – No, M. Bougran, it just won't do. You can keep that old office skivvy, and get *him* to rub you down with a flannel to ease your rheumatism and some of that ointment that stinks of fresh paint: *I'm* leaving! I'm not going to be treated like this, at my age!'

M. Bougran looked at her, dumbfounded.

'But look here, Eulalie my dear, don't get angry like that: come on, if you like I'll raise your wages a bit…'

'My wages! Oh no, don't think I'd stay for the fifty francs a month you're offering me now; if I want to leave, it's because of the way you're behaving towards me!'

The thought crossed M. Bougran's mind that he hadn't at all offered to give her a wage of fifty francs, he had simply intended to raise her present wage by five francs a month; but faced with the old woman's wrathful countenance as she declared that she was going to leave in spite of everything, he bowed his head and made excuses, trying to soft-talk her with wheedling compliments, and get her to stay rather than packing her bags as she was threatening.

'And where will you put him, then? Not in my kitchen, I hope!' asked Eulalie who, having obtained what she wanted, consented to calm down.

'No, in the hallway; you won't need to bother about him, or even see him; as you see, dearie, there was no need to fly off the handle the way you did!'

'I'll fly off the handle if I want to! And don't you try and tell me what to do!' she cried, getting back onto her high horse: she had decided to stay, but she wasn't going to put up with even these mild reproaches.

Worn out, M. Bougran didn't dare look at her as she strutted out of the room with insolent pride.

4

'Not much in the post this morning!'

'No, Huriot, we're falling behind; I had an important piece of business to deal with yesterday, and as I have to do it all by myself, I had to leave the less urgent questions to one side, and the service is suffering in consequence!'

'We're turning into real slackers, as poor old Monsieur de Pinaudel used to say. Did you know him, Monsieur?'

'Yes, old chap, I did. Oh, he was a very able man. He was in a class of his own when it came to composing a tricky letter. Another trusty civil servant that they retired prematurely, like me!'

'Yes, and you should just look at the service these days: young whippersnappers who have only one thing on their minds – how to have a good time! Ah, Monsieur Bougran, office life isn't what it used to be!'

M. Bougran sighed. Then he dismissed his assistant with a nod and settled back down to work.

Ah, this administrative jargon he had to get right! All those turns of phrase: 'our client pleads'; 'in reply to your kind letter, I have the honour to inform you that'; 'as per the opinion expressed in your dispatch relative to...' Those customary idioms: 'the spirit, if not the letter of the law', 'giving all due weight to the importance of the considerations to which you refer in support of this argument...' And finally, those formulae destined for the Ministry of Justice, in which reference was made to 'the opinion emanating from His Chancellery', all those evasive and inconclusive phrases: 'I am inclined to believe', or, 'it will not have escaped your notice', or, 'I would be most grateful if' – that whole vocabulary and phraseology going back to the age of Colbert, gave

M. Bougran a terrible headache.

His head in his clenched hands, he reread the first sentences he had just drafted. At present he was engaged in highly specialised exercises, up to his neck in an appeal to the Council of State.

And he falteringly murmured the inevitable formula of address:

'Monsieur le Président,
The Legal Department has passed on to me, for deliberation, an appeal brought before the Council of State by M. So-and-So, with the aim of annulling as ultra vires *my decision dated the...'*

And the second sentence:

'Before passing to a discussion of the arguments brought forward by the petitioner in support of his case, I will summarily recall the facts that motivate the present appeal.'

It was here that it started to get difficult.

'I ought to spend some time packaging it, and not move forward too hastily,' M. Bougran muttered. 'M. So-and-So's request is well founded in law. We'll have to try and wriggle our way out of this dispute, go in for a bit of sharp practice, deliberately overlook certain points. All in all, the letter of the law gives me forty days to reply: I have time to think about it, mull it over in my head, not leap blindly to the defence of the ministry...'

'More post!' said Huriot, bringing two new letters.

'*More?* It's been a hard day – and it's already four o'clock!'

'All the same, it's amazing how that Huriot reeks of garlic

and wine,' Bougran said to himself, drawing a deep breath of fresh air once the assistant had gone out. 'Just like in the office!' – he added with satisfaction. 'And there's dust everywhere; he never bothers to sweep – again, just like in the office. It's so authentic!'

What was equally authentic, though he barely noticed it, was the growing antagonism between Eulalie and Huriot. Even though she had obtained her fifty francs per month, the maid couldn't get used to this drunkard, even though he was obliging and mild-mannered and slept on a chair in the hallway, waiting for his employee to ring for him.

'Lazy sod,' she would say, shifting her copper pots and pans round; 'when you think that old office skivvy snores away all day long doing nothing!'

And to demonstrate her discontent to her master, she deliberately spoilt the sauces, refused to utter a word, and violently slammed the doors.

Timidly, M. Bougran would lower his eyes, and close his ears to the terrible rows that took place between his two domestics at the kitchen door. Nonetheless, he could not help but pick up the odd phrase in which, for once united in their opinions, Eulalie and Huriot called him a 'madman', a 'feather-brain', an 'old idiot'.

This filled him with a sadness that had a negative influence on his work. He could no longer settle down and get on with it. Even though he would have needed all the concentration of which he was capable to draw up this appeal, he found that his mind wandered in the most extravagant way; his thoughts kept returning to dwell on those domestic quarrels, on Eulalie's ferocious bad temper, and as he tried to disarm her with the imploring meekness of his sheepish gaze, she stood even more on her dignity, sure of being able to win if she struck hard. And he, in despair, stayed at home by himself in the evenings, chewing on his disgusting evening meal, not daring to complain.

All this aggravation accelerated the infirmities of age that were now starting to weigh him down; he had rushes of blood to the head, found he got breathless after his meals, and at night kept waking in a cold sweat.

Soon he found it difficult to make his way downstairs and leave the building so as to 'go to his office'; but he stiffened his resolve, setting out each morning in spite of everything, taking a half-hour walk before returning home.

His poor head was spinning; all the same, he wore out his strength on this appeal that he had embarked on and from which he could no longer extricate himself. With great tenacity, when he felt his mind clearer, he continued to labour over that fictitious problem he had set himself.

He did resolve it, finally, but he so overexerted himself mentally that his brain gave way and he suffered a fit. He cried aloud. Neither Huriot nor the maid bothered to come. Around evening they found him, slumped over the table, his lips muttering disconnectedly, his eyes vacant. They sent for a doctor who diagnosed apoplexy and declared that there was no hope for him.

M. Bougran died that night, while his assistant and his maid exchanged insults and tried to dodge each other so that they could slip off and ransack the drawers.

On the desk of the now deserted office lay the sheet of paper on which M. Bougran, sensing that he was about to die, had hastily scrawled the last lines of his appeal:

'For these reasons I cannot, M. le Président, but express a negative opinion on the action to be taken in the case of the appeal lodged by M. So-and-So.'

NOTES

1. Bullier's was a well-known Parisian dancehall (opened 1842).
2. Messidor was a month in the French Revolutionary calendar (mid-June to mid-July).
3. Victor Cherbuliez (1829–99) and Octave Feuillet (1821–90) were popular contemporary writers.
4. Moustiers: a town known for its faience-ware.
5. These were operas: *Richard Coeur-de-Lion* (1784) by André Grétry (1741–1813), *Le Pré-aux-Clercs* (1832) by Ferdinand Hérold (1791–1833).
6. Constant Coquelin (1841–1909) was a famous actor, as was his brother Ernest (1848–1909).
7. Adriaen van Ostade (1610–85) and the two Teniers, David Teniers the Elder (1582–1649) and his son David Teniers the Younger (1610–90), were realist/genre painters.
8. Messidor (see note 2 above); Ventôse was mid-February to mid-March in the same calendar.

Joris-Karl Huysmans was born in 1848. At the age of eighteen he went to work for the Ministry of the Interior in Paris, and published his first article, in *La Revue Mensuelle*, a year later. For the next thirty years, this odd but evidently fruitful combination – of the humdrum routine of government service and the saving grace of fiction – would resonate throughout Huysmans' work.

Early on in his literary career, Huysmans declared that his model of a perfect writer was Emile Zola. In 1877 he publicly endorsed Zola's 'bourgeois' realism – which had come under attack in literary circles – in a series of articles. The endorsement is reflected in those parts of Huysmans' own work which scrutinise the unglamorous tedium of contemporary existence. But Huysmans' varied oeuvre also encompassed more recherché tastes, first in the occult arts and the macabre, and later in religion. If it was Christianity which personally affected Huysmans most profoundly, it was his treatment of the occult which was to make his fortune and his name. Huysmans researched the themes of his best-selling 'black book', *Là-Bas* (1891), in person, with the help of his mistress, Berthe Courrière, and its popularity with the reading public enabled him to retire from the ministry in 1898. *Là-Bas* was followed by his 'white book', *En Route* (1895), in which he began an exploration of Catholicism that would sustain him for the rest of his life.

Huysmans quickly became a fêted writer in Parisian literary circles. In 1896, he helped found the famous Académie Goncourt; in 1907 he was made an Officer of the Legion of Honour; and such was his popularity in Paris at the time of his death that a huge crowd followed his funeral procession from Notre-Dame-des-Champs, to the cemetery at Montparnasse where he was buried. Huysmans' writing was quickly canonised in France, and he remains one of the most important figures of nineteenth-century European literature.

Andrew Brown studied at the University of Cambridge, where he taught French for many years. He now works as a freelance teacher and translator. He is the author of *Roland Barthes: the Figures of Writing* (OUP, 1993) and his translations include Zola's *For a Night of Love*, Gautier's *The Jinx*, Hoffmann's *Mademoiselle de Scudéri*, Gide's *Theseus*, de Sade's *Incest*, Schiller's *The Ghost-seer*, Balzac's *Colonel Chabert*, Stendhal's *Memoirs of an Egotist*, and Maupassant's *Butterball*, all published by Hesperus Press.

HESPERUS PRESS – 100 PAGES

Hesperus Press, as suggested by the Latin motto, is committed to bringing near what is far – far both in space and time. Works written by the greatest authors, and unjustly neglected or simply little known in the English-speaking world, are made accessible through new translations and a completely fresh editorial approach. Through these short classic works, each around 100 pages in length, the reader will be introduced to the greatest writers from all times and all cultures.

For more information on Hesperus Press, please visit our website: **www.hesperuspress.com**

ET REMOTISSIMA PROPE

SELECTED TITLES FROM HESPERUS PRESS

Gustave Flaubert *Memoirs of a Madman*
Alexander Pope *Scriblerus*
Ugo Foscolo *Last Letters of Jacopo Ortis*
Anton Chekhov *The Story of a Nobody*
Joseph von Eichendorff *Life of a Good-for-nothing*
Mark Twain *The Diary of Adam and Eve*
Giovanni Boccaccio *Life of Dante*
Victor Hugo *The Last Day of a Condemned Man*
Joseph Conrad *Heart of Darkness*
Edgar Allan Poe *Eureka*
Emile Zola *For a Night of Love*
Daniel Defoe *The King of Pirates*
Giacomo Leopardi *Thoughts*
Nikolai Gogol *The Squabble*
Franz Kafka *Metamorphosis*
Herman Melville *The Enchanted Isles*
Leonardo da Vinci *Prophecies*
Charles Baudelaire *On Wine and Hashish*
William Makepeace Thackeray *Rebecca and Rowena*
Wilkie Collins *Who Killed Zebedee?*
Théophile Gautier *The Jinx*
Charles Dickens *The Haunted House*
Luigi Pirandello *Loveless Love*
Fyodor Dostoevsky *Poor People*
E.T.A. Hoffmann *Mademoiselle de Scudéri*
Henry James *In the Cage*
Francis Petrarch *My Secret Book*
André Gide *Theseus*
D.H. Lawrence *The Fox*
Percy Bysshe Shelley *Zastrozzi*
Marquis de Sade *Incest*
Oscar Wilde *The Portrait of Mr W.H.*
Giacomo Casanova *The Duel*
Leo Tolstoy *Hadji Murat*
Friedrich von Schiller *The Ghost-seer*
Nathaniel Hawthorne *Rappaccini's Daughter*
Pietro Aretino *The School of Whoredom*
Honoré de Balzac *Colonel Chabert*
Thomas Hardy *Fellow-Townsmen*
Arthur Conan Doyle *The Tragedy of the Korosko*
Stendhal *Memoirs of an Egotist*
Katherine Mansfield *In a German Pension*
Giovanni Verga *Life in the Country*
Ivan Turgenev *Faust*
Theodor Storm *The Lake of the Bees*
F. Scott Fitzgerald *The Rich Boy*
Dante Alighieri *New Life*
Guy de Maupassant *Butterball*
Charlotte Brontë *The Green Dwarf*
Elizabeth Gaskell *Lois the Witch*
Joris-Karl Huysmans *With the Flow*
George Eliot *Amos Barton*
Gabriele D'Annunzio *The Book of the Virgins*
Alexander Pushkin *Dubrovsky*